# TO CLIMB A
# FLAT
# MOUNTAIN

by
G. David Nordley

# TO CLIMB A
# FLAT
# MOUNTAIN

Publishing History
Analog Magazine, Nov/Dec 2009

First published in 2012 by Variations on a Theme

Cover design: Brief Candle Press

First Brief Candle Press edition published 2015
www.briefcandlepress.com

ISBN: 978-1-942319-06-1

*This book is dedicated to my*
*mentor and friend, Algis Budrys*

# ACKNOWLEDGMENTS

I would first like to thank Whensday People Mike van Pelt, Candy Lowe, Sandra Saidak, Frank Wu, Jim Aiken, Sarah Stegall, Robin Riversmith, Deirdre Moen, Adrienne Gormley, Dio Sanchez, Jason Stewart, Aleks Haecky and Gabi Haecky for their reading time and comments. More thanks go to Stan Schmidt for his comments and for buying the serial version. My special thanks to my wife, Gayle Wiesner for all the proofreading. And finally, thanks to Deb Houdek for making this edition possible.

# CHAPTER 1
# SOMEWHERE UNEXPECTED

Jacques Song opened his eyes and saw a huge fish floating above the canopy of his cold sleep unit and staring at him. He shut them immediately; it must be a bad dream. People often had dreams as cold sleep evolved into normal sleep and wakefulness.

Last night, 21 June 2345, he and the rest of the corps had listened to some inspirational nonsense from Earth Empress Marie, lifted a glass of rum spiked with cold sleep preparation drugs, and dutifully lain down on their hotel beds at Sheffield Station in Earth orbit.

In deep sleep, they'd been transferred to Cold Sleep Units and loaded onto starships bound for 36 Ophiuchi. The process would be reversed twenty-three years later when the invasion force had established itself, hopefully undetected, at a base in the Kuiper belt around 36 Ophiuchi A and B. Their mission was to liberate a colony gone horrifically wrong.

But that colony was not under a sea filled with staring fish.

The colony leaders didn't believe in using robots–labor cleansed the soul. Slavery in all but name had evolved in a decade. Polygamy, child marriage, gladiatorial executions and inherited subordinate status became the rule. They'd bungled relations with primitive aliens on another of 36 Ophiuchi A's planets, raising concerns about humanity's status in the galaxy.

But those aliens did not, as he remembered, look like fish.

Dissenters had fled to the hills and risked everything to call for help–which would take half a century at best to get there. Before 36 Ophiuchi, the consensus had been that the distance between stars made interstellar warfare impossible. The colony leaders had counted on it.

But faced with a cry for help, Earth considered the impossible. There'd been a mammoth debate informed by massive simulations showing that, absent outside influence, the theocracy might persist indefinitely. The decision had been made, volunteers recruited, and robots instructed to prepare a fleet. Jacques, divorced and looking for distance, had signed up.

Jacques opened his eyes again, and the fish was still there, all too real. Maybe two meters long, it boasted a huge parrot-like beak, but otherwise looked something like a shark. He was wide awake now. He was obviously not on the conveyor ship, *Resolution,* so something *else* had gone horrifically wrong.

He tried to touch the net, but the lack of response didn't surprise him. The CSU seemed inert, but he was breathing, so it must be functioning to some extent. The things were designed to keep you viable in a suspended state for a couple of centuries without external power–they warmed you up to a coma every few months for DNA repair.

"CSU, what's your energy level?" he asked. As soon as he moved, the parrot-beaked shark tried to bite through the canopy, but didn't have much success against the flexidiamond.

A heads-up display flashed in front of him, superposing itself over the curious–or hungry–fish. It showed he had about two hours left at present consumption levels, which were at emergency minimum. The display flashed off again. The CSU may as well have said, "I've done what I can. It's your problem now."

Jacques raised himself on his elbows. The water–assuming it was water–around him was not all that clear and the light level must be very low. From what he could see, his CSU seemed to be resting on nearly level sand, with a few huge dark boulder-like objects here and there. The surface seemed far above him.

He would probably have to try to reach it.

But when? Conventional wisdom would have him wait as long as he could for rescue. The CSU, he realized, had maximized that time. Rescue wasn't coming.

First things first. He needed to inventory his assets. He reached into a cubbyhole to his left for his personal effects, his wrist comp and a couple of backup data disks—what he'd left on his hotel night table for the Resolution's robots to take with him. The objects seemed very light—low gravity?

The wrist comp was dead, powerless. He shivered. Just how long had it been? He suppressed the urge to ask immediately—if he were going to get out of this situation alive, he would need to use what was left of the CSU's power very efficiently.

Another cubbyhole held an emergency kit in a sealable bag, which he emptied and inventoried. It struck him as an eclectic jumble of stuff someone assembled to fill a regulatory square, never expected to be used. There was another wrist comp, its memory filled, no doubt, with all sorts of survival information. It was powerless. There was a survival tent, nicely folded down to the size of an envelope. There were a few pieces of primitive, non-electronic gear including a dozen nutrition bars, a compass, a magnifying lens, needle and thread, a ten-centimeter long multitool, a pair of fabric canteens, a photovoltaic power supply, binoculars, space blankets, etc. Finally, occupying most of the volume of the kit, there was a shipsuit.

Even in the low gravity, struggling into the last was not easy in the coffin-like space in the CSU, but once he got his legs in, his body heat began to power the smart fabric up and it relaxed to make the rest of the job easier. It molded itself around his body like a second skin, except for the hood. The latter had a transparent section that could seal up for vacuum use. Hopefully, it would work as well underwater.

It also had an emergency life support pack. For a moment, Jacques smiled. It could make oxygen; he could wait several hours more to try his escape, using that to breathe. Then he found it was powerless as well. He sighed; many of the suit's functions could be powered by his own body heat and movements, but not that.

That was all he had. He imagined that, should he survive and return to Earth some centuries hence, some of these objects might be displayed in a museum as quaint relics of bygone pioneers.

Okay, it was time to find out where he was, what it was like outside, and what had happened. He told the CSU to power up. The first thing he got was text telling him that video was down for power conservation.

To the first question, the CSU told him they were at an unsurveyed red dwarf, IRO 031010.36485, on a planet with a breathable atmosphere that the Resolution had found 628 light years from Earth! On the Earth calendar, it was Tuesday, the 23rd of March in the year 3521.

That was almost 1000 years from when they had departed. He made himself cope with that as an objective fact; he would deal with the emotional reality later. Humanity was still in the very early stages of biological immortality. Had been, he corrected himself. They'd probably worked things out by now. Some friends might still be alive, active, even looking for him. But the gap in time would be as large as the gap between Marie's ceremonial monarchy and Charlemagne. He could deal with it later, he repeated to himself. For now, he had to survive.

So the *Resolution* had not decelerated at 36 Ophiuchi–the beamrider's nightmare. Starships were pushed to relativistic velocities riding on a beam of microscopic pellets from their departure system, which they ionized and reflected with magnetic fields. To decelerate, they normally relied on a prepositioned pellet stream. Somehow, this hadn't happened.

For the invasion, the first units into the system had carried enough mass to decelerate on their own. These passed by the system and decelerated on the far side, their bulk shielding their exhaust from observation. Once in 36 Ophiuchi's Kuiper belt, they'd made deceleration trails for the rest of the fleet. The whole process had taken an agonizing half century.

The CSU told him the lasers used to guide the nanopellets to the starship had been replaced with a dummy load. Almost all of the pellets passed by the starship without slowing it down. Who or what had done that, and when, was unknown.

There were contingency plans for failure to decelerate. The starship had coasted until it found a habitable planet it could reach and then implemented an emergency deceleration protocol, deploying a superconducting loop several kilometers across to drag against the interstellar medium until it had reached a hundredth of lightspeed or so, and then going into rocket mode, using its auxiliary nuclear power units while sacrificing its water, redundant structure, invasion stores, and lithium hydride shielding, for fuel. It almost made it; but ended up 103 kilometers per second short, and had to try aerocapture.

Starships were tough, but not designed to function in a planetary atmosphere. Its breakup would have absorbed the worst of the reentry forces, perhaps controlled well enough to spill its cargo of CSUs into a shallow body of water. There were three atmospheric shuttles. They weren't designed for that much aerobraking. But if one or two survived on autopilot, Jacques thought, that could make all the difference in survival. The odds weren't good for the CSU occupants either, but with a layer of ice, maybe. That was the best the ship could do.

The CSU went silent and Jacques reflected. Interstellar warfare was "impossible" until the horror of what was happening in the 36 Ophiuchi system made Earth try it anyway. Perhaps they'd been right in the first place.

The parrot-beaked shark, making no concession to human biological immortality, had not gone away. It was, he decided, definitely hungry. So was he—his cells needed to repair the radiation damage since his last CSU cycle, and that took energy. Cosmic rays could be dealt with by shielding, but carbon 14 was part of you. He ate four of the dozen nutrition bars, knowing that he might regret the binge later, but thinking it was a good thing to do while he was momentarily safe and secure. As he ate he eyed the parrot-beaked shark, thinking filet. This eating thing works both ways, fella, he thought with a grin.

He would have to flood the CSU, he realized, to equalize pressure and get the canopy off. That would likely render his last link with technological civilization inoperable. There was irony in that; his expertise was in dealing with artificial intelligences and subsentient systems.

"Can you still record?" he asked it.

[Yes] appeared in the heads-up display.

In a few short sentences, he explained who he was and how he'd gotten there, and left notes for any of his fellow passengers in the unlikely event they might find his CSU.

"Make as many copies of that as you have room for."

[Done]

Jacques stuck the emergency kit bag on a geckro patch on his suit. He was ready as he could get; there was no reason to delay longer. His heart pounding, he chanted to make himself relax and use less oxygen. After a couple of minutes, he felt at peace and ready. If his life were to end now, so be it.

"Release the fasteners on both sides of the canopy. Give me pure oxygen–exhaust what you've stored. Then flood the unit." He took more deep breaths as cold water rose rapidly on either side of him. The pressure equalized with his face not ten centimeters between him and the fish's beak. It lunged repeatedly, its blows booming on the canopy.

He sealed his hood without trapping a lot of water in with him, then pushed the canopy off and, grasping it by both edges, stood up. If the fish had sense enough to swim around it, he was done for, but it just kept trying to push through what it couldn't see–a stalemate that would end as soon as he ran out of breath, because the canopy was too heavy to carry to the surface.

He looked down at the empty CSU and smiled to himself. It was easy enough to flip the canopy around between fish attacks and then stand on the edge of the CSU and lean so that the fish was below him. With a now-or-never shove, he pushed the canopy down onto the CSU with parrot-beak still trying to swim through it. With it trapped inside, he swam for the surface.

Judging crudely from the change in volume of air in the CSU, the pressure was something like eight atmospheres at the bottom, the equivalent of eighty meters deep on Earth. But the surface proved much farther away than that. Despite starting with several liters of oxygen in his hood, he was groggy by the time he broke the surface of the water. He pulled off the hood and took a gasping first breath.

He felt almost instantly restored as he bobbed up and down in steep waves; it took remarkably little effort to keep his body high out of the water. At the crest of a wave, he got a view of his surroundings. He'd emerged from a freshwater lake, not a sea, but it was a large one, with distant hills just barely sticking up over the horizon. Hills surrounded the lake without a discernible gap–a caldera, from the steepness of the walls next to him. He saw no vegetation.

Remembering that the parrot-beaked shark might have relatives, he swam for the nearest shore at about a stroke per second. Strangely, he didn't tire and even increased his pace a bit.

The shore proved rocky, and the rocks looked volcanic and sharp, 'a-'a lava, he thought. The waves were impressively high. Still, he felt very strong, much stronger than he should after coming out of cold sleep.

Bobbing along in the waves, parallel to the shore, he eventually found a beach that was more gravel than rock and approached it slowly, feet dangling beneath him. His feet touched briefly, then he was swept back again. He rode the next wave in and got enough purchase with hands and feet to hold on through the backwash. Then he scrambled forward ahead of the next wave.

He stood on the shore breathing easily—not panting despite what should have been heavy exercise. He was fit; all expedition personnel had gotten many hours of hypergravity training, but his lack of distress still surprised him. Gravity was clearly much lower than on Earth here, even less than on Mars, he guessed. The sky was high and gray, there had to be a sun somewhere, but it wasn't immediately apparent where it was. It was decidedly warm and humid.

Okay, the first thing to do was to plug one of his wrist comps into the photovoltaic power supply and see if anyone else were around. He spread out the flexible array, almost a meter square, and plugged the adapter into his wrist comp, or tried to. It didn't fit! Damning his luck and wondering why, after three centuries or so of electronics manufacture, such things weren't standardized, he reached for the wrist comp from the emergency kit. That would *have* to fit.

It did, but nothing happened. A broken wire? Or had something in the electronics of either device not survived a millennium of neglect? The batteries in the wrist comps were likely suspects. Or, he thought, layers of atoms in contact in various transistors and diodes may have interpenetrated each other through some kind of Brownian motion so they no longer functioned. He'd never had occasion to inquire about the lifetime of such devices and, of course, there was now nothing to ask. If he was going to survive, it would have to be on his wits alone.

He took stock; however great he felt right now, he had only eight nutrition bars left to eat. He had no clothing except for the emergency suit that he wore. There were clearly fishlike things in the caldera, and if they were edible, he might be able to catch enough to survive—thought he wasn't sure how, having never fished in his life. For shelter, since the area was obviously volcanic in origin, there should be lava tubes.

Was his the only CSU to make it? He should look for other survivors. Names of classmates slotted for the Resolution ran through his mind. They weren't soldiers; their job was to reconstruct and reeducate the colony after the theocrats had been displaced. Most, he had known only since Annapolis, but he'd grown up with Edith Lu, Huong Devieux, and Ted Blackwell in metropolitan Port Moresby sixty years ago—make that something like 1060 years ago.

He scanned the lake with its strange high waves and impassable lava block shore line.

Face reality, Jacques, he told himself. He was in no position to find and rescue anyone. He had to find food, and that meant getting out of the caldera. He would come back. There was likely a large variance in CSU survival time; no one else was likely to need help right now.

Everything caught up with him then; his impossible situation, the unfairness of it all, the totalitarian monsters that had been the cause of the expedition and its likely sabotage, the great decision makers of the Interplanetary Association senate who sent others to take their risks and clean up for their failures of imagination, and the minimum effort logic of those who put only a dozen nutrition bars in a CSU emergency kit... He screamed. The screams echoed from the barren lava cliffs.

When he recovered himself, he decided to do something to defy the fate that sent him here, to make some mark on the universe that was trying to kill him. He could make a pile of rocks, a cairn. Practically, it would help him find the spot again. It was no work at all in the low gravity to build a stack as tall as he was.

The lava wasn't all 'a-'a. Here and there were rivers of smooth pahoehoe, some of which had fragmented into relatively flat shards. He brushed one off and using another, smaller fragment, sketched the shoreline, and scratched where he thought the sunken CSU lay. Under that he scratched his name and the date. Then, after a moment of thought, he added "= Day 0."

# CHAPTER 2
# AT THE RIM OF THE WORLD

The cliffs turned out to be not as barren as he thought. Here and there, small trees had begun to colonize the caldera wall–he hadn't recognized them because their leaves were a very dark blue green–almost black–and indistinguishable from the lava. The higher he got, the bigger the trees, and the bare rock between them became covered with dark soil.

In a rare level clearing, he tripped and righted himself easily in the low gravity. The culprit was a ground vine with dark, grass-like leaves. I'll call it "tanglegrass," he thought with a frown. At the clearing edge was a thirty-meter tree. He tested its bark with a blade from his multitool; it was very soft and wet, maybe waterlogged–not like a tree at all, but rather more like ice plant.

Was the pulp of the tree edible? It should, of course, be thoroughly tested and analyzed. He laughed at that notion and cut out a finger-sized piece, bit off a little, and spat it out. Acidic, bitter, and with an odor of rotten flesh–he would have to be very, very hungry to try to eat that. He washed the taste out with water from the fabric canteen. That was Earth water, he thought, from a thousand years ago. He ought to treat it with reverence.

No, get hold of yourself, he told himself. Water was water.

It was getting noticeably dark, though not noticeably cooler. Here and there around the roots of the bitterwood tree were pockets of sand and gravel that were reasonably soft and level. He made camp.

The next day he reached the rim of the caldera in early morning. It was anomalously clear when he worked his way around a last boulder to the relatively flat top. The red dwarf sun appeared noticeably larger than Sol in a sky that seemed a somewhat lighter shade of blue. A few more steps took him clear of the brush and rocks.

What he saw made no sense to him–a vast triangular plain stretched out before him, its sides converging to an impossibly distant vertex ahead of him. The plain was divided into great fuzzy arcs of color–gray, white, red, black, green, blue and green again–apparently centered on himself, with the outermost almost tangent to the triangle's sides.

To his left, haze and clouds obscured the distant view, but to his right, through breaks in high creamy clouds, he thought he could glimpse a repetition of the pattern in front of him. Apparently, the planet had at least two huge conical volcanoes, as perfect in form as Mount Fuji, and so high that they extended beyond the limits of what must be a very extended atmosphere. Could they be in isostatic equilibrium? He shook his head; such calculations would need to be put off for now.

Immediately below him was the rocky mountainside, mostly bare but dotted with trees. Below that was a dark green forest. That yielded to a sea or a very wide river. Beyond its misty, distant shore was another very dark band; probably more forest. That thinned out to a band of lighter green, which merged into a ruddy brown. The last complete arc was white. Beyond that, banding the base of the remaining tip of the triangle were bands of distant clouds. The peak itself was almost geometrically sharp, a dark lunar gray, and apparently cratered.

Scanning the edge of the forest, he spotted a trail, a narrow and very Earth-like path leading down into the forest. What had made it? Other survivors? Natives or local animals? Something edible? Something dangerous?

Well, he had best get going. On the way, something crunched under his foot. It looked for all the world like a piece of curved green and black mottled plastic. If it had been part of a sphere, the whole thing might be half a meter in diameter. Was it part of a broken lava bubble? An eggshell? Of what monster, if so? But there was no time to spend on these questions. Survival called and he would have to concentrate on the trail.

The scale of the trees became evident as he descended. The largest were easily a hundred meters tall and five across; like California redwoods. These trees were not at all like the bitterwood tree he had cut into earlier; their wood was dark and suitably woody. They had a bark of sorts, black, smooth, and chitinous in the mature trees, with longitudinal ridges that seemed to run the length of the tree. He decided to call it blackwood, and cut a sapling for a hiking pole and a potential defensive staff.

As he looked carefully, he saw evidence of frequent fire. The darkness of the soil, the great space between the trees—there was a very open feeling to this forest. There was no brush taller than he was, and much of that was composed of immature bitterwood and blackwood. Everything seemed soft—no thorns or scratchy plants.

He came across a running brook and filled his canteen, fine bubbles foaming out of its neck filter. It was only half Earth water now. If he never emptied it, there would always still be some molecules from the home planet in that canteen, in ever decreasing proportion, of course. He considered boiling it, but time was pressing. The filter would catch the microbes and his enhanced immunological system would be pretty tough on viruses that hadn't co-evolved with terrestrial life.

Out of the corner of his eye, he caught something scurrying away from the trail, a kind of furry ball with red and black markings that seemed to have too many legs. Why would it be afraid of him? There must be something about his size and shape that was dangerous. He thought about lashing his multitool to a blackwood sapling spear, with its blade deployed. But if he lost that tool!

Given the volcanic nature of the hillside, there should be some obsidian around, but he didn't know what to look for, nor did he have any confidence in his ability to whack raw obsidian into a spear point. Then his eyes fell on a dead blackwood branch. He scrambled off the path to pick it up. The bark had dried into plastic-like hardness. When he scraped out the rest of the rotten pulpwood, he was left with a hard, hollow cylinder. He cut one end of this at a steep angle and jammed the other over the end of his walking stick. Then, with the ludicrous image of himself as a Pleistocene hunter in his head, he threw the improvised spear into a bitterwood tree.

It sank in with a satisfying thwump. He made three more slanted cylindrical spear points, put them in his emergency kit bag, and continued his descent.

In his second day down the mountainside, ravenously hungry, with only five nutrition bars left, he decided whatever he was doing was not working. He was seriously thinking of the fish trapped in the CSU—could he find it again, dive down and kill the fish? It had been big—maybe a hundred kilos of meat on it. He should have taken that opportunity when he was there.

Okay, he wasn't going to just run into something to eat walking down the trail. Why not try setting up a blind and watching for what might come by? He could give that a day.

It was a long boring day, but that evening something did come by. It seemed vaguely like a cross between a kangaroo and a dinosaur so he mentally dubbed it a kangasaur. It was at least twice his height, and its head bobbed from side to side. Jacques readied his spear, then got a look at the fierce claws on the kangasaur's feet and thought better of it. It stared in his direction, but he stayed perfectly still. It ambled over to a bitterwood tree, reached up about as far as its neck would extend, and worried away at something under a bitterwood leaf. Then it left.What had it found? Could he climb a bitterwood tree? Their lowest branches were about three meters up and the bark, though not as slick as the shiny blackwood bark, was still very smooth. But gravity was low. An experimental leap up brought his eye level perhaps six meters above the forest floor. He jumped for a branch, clumsily slung himself under it, sloth-like, and shinnied out to look under its leaves. It was barren; he would have to climb higher than he could leap.

Jacques remembered going to an art museum with his class in which he'd seen a picture of a man climbing a tree with rope around the trunk, holding himself to the bark that way. There was a coil of carbon-nanofiber twine in the emergency kit, 100 meters according to the label.

It took some experimentation and a couple of falls, but the next morning Jacques made it up a bitterwood tree and looked under its leaves. He had to go higher than the first level of branches, but finally discovered a cluster of teardrop-shaped fruits. The rind was tough, but no match for the steel of his multitool blade, and he got at the pulp beneath.

He knew the risks, but he had to find something edible. He nibbled at it. It was mostly soft fibers, almost like pasta, and relatively flavorless; nothing sharp, bitter, or otherwise deadly seeming. Ten minutes after the first taste, he took a mouthful. It seemed to go down okay.

He put a couple fruits in his kit bag, which was beginning to become stuffed, and dropped down to the ground. He would wait a day to see how his body reacted before eating more. He camped by a brook, sealed in his tent despite the warm humidity of the place, and slept fitfully.

The next day, not having gotten sick, he ate the whole thing, minus the hard seeds toward the center of the fruit. So far so good, he thought, and headed downhill.

Part of the apparent flatness of the landscape from the caldera rim, he realized, was because the trees got taller as he descended. As a guess, the tallest blackwoods were almost three hundred meters high and five meters across. He felt like a squirrel in a forest of giant sequoia. Their oval leaves were longer than he was tall, with stiff hollow veins and webbing like sheets of felted canvas. Picking one up, he felt like an ant, able to lift several times his own body mass.

By the end of the day, he was still healthy. With food, he could survive. Under a leaf lean-to, cushioned by soft loam, he lay down. The next thing he knew, morning had arrived.

# CHAPTER 3
# THE KILLER APE

Deeper into the forest, rocks had become fewer and fewer; the floor was a rich, soft loam. His cairns were now teepees of fallen blackwood branches. Over the next week, he taught himself to weave a passable basket out of blackwood saplings, discovered a thin fibrous green vine that was surprisingly strong, found a mildly sweet edible berry to break the monotony of bitterwood fruit, found a hollow "flute plant" that grew perfectly straight but no higher than about a meter, and identified six native animals, including the furry spider-like thing he'd seen on his first day. But he was getting increasingly tired–bitterwood fruit and berries alone might not be an adequate diet.

The furry spider-like things–he decided to call them hirachnoids–foraged on a mushroom-like plant that grew beneath fallen blackwood tree leaves. He didn't try eating those–not a rational decision considering all the other chances he was taking, but eating things that looked like mushrooms made him nervous. He gathered up some of these and put them under his basket, weighted it down with a hunk of lava, then propped it up with a twig, to which he attached a string, the idea being to pull the twig out when the furry spider-like thing was underneath the basket.

This didn't work well–the little animals were able to skitter out before the rim fell. That, he realized, was a consequence of the low gravity–no matter how much weight you put on something it would only fall so fast. If he could only *push* it down... The answer was a long fallen blackwood branch resting on the top of the trap. The trick was to pull the string attached to the stick first and step on the branch immediately afterward: one, two. If his timing was ever so slightly off and the pressure from the lever came first, the stick wouldn't come out at all, but if he left too much time between string and foot, the critter would escape.

After a couple of tries, he caught one. Up close, it actually looked very spider-like, with compound eyes, but six instead of eight legs and seemingly no segments–a big hairy ball maybe half a meter across. Its mouth irised open like an anus to allow a forked appendage to shoot out and grab pieces of the mushroom-like plant. It was big–maybe half a meter in diameter. Despite being trapped, it ignored him and worked away at eating the bait.

Jacques hesitated. He had never killed anything before. But he had only two nutrition bars left. He needed to survive, and to survive he would probably need protein. Protein meant meat because he had no way of determining if the vegetation had any. Still it was all guesswork; he didn't know that killing this thing would solve his problem. He didn't know how smart it was, whether it would suffer, or even retaliate in some very effective way. He pondered this for several minutes, then put one of his spear tips on his walking stick and struck the thing hard right between the eyes. It collapsed immediately.

Dissection proved a problem; the hirachnoid's hair was as stiff and bristly as it looked and longer than the blade of his multitool knife. He ended up lashing the multitool to a flute plant shaft with green twine and going at it whaler-style. The first cut produced not meat, but a fountain of mucous yellow ichor that stank like rotten eggs. He almost gagged, then recovering himself, made another cut.

Suddenly, the creature's corpse began to pulsate and flop around. Jacques recoiled in disgust. Then out of the cut, a procession of miniature hirachnoids emerged–miniatures of the first except for a lack of hair. Jacques' stomach began to get queasy, especially when the little ones dragged pieces of their mother's–or their host's– innards out of the incision and ate them.

Sickened, Jacques backed away from the trap and sat down to collect himself. Periodically, thereafter, he checked the trap.

By evening, nothing was left of the hirachnoid but the skin and legs. He held a leg up–it was tough and horny, like a crab leg, and felt massive enough to contain some meat. He gathered the other legs and took them back to his camp by the brook. Using some stones, he cracked one open and found some white fibrous meat inside; obviously the leg muscle.

He pulled it out, cut a small piece off with his blade, washed it in the creek and tasted it. It was extraordinarily rich and tasted somewhat like buttered lobster, but was much softer than he remembered lobster being–indeed it seemed to melt in his mouth.

Jackpot, he thought. Maybe. Would the rest keep until morning? He should wait to make sure nothing untoward happened to him as a result of his bite, but it was too good. He took another bite, then, in an act of incredible self control, he wrapped the remainder in leaves and sealed it in his emergency kit bag. There was no room for the other legs, so he put them in the basket and hung that by a rope from a branch.

Then he improvised a hammock with green twine and bitterwood leaves and went to sleep.

He woke up with the first light, feeling better than he had in days. The remaining part of the first leg didn't smell right after sitting overnight, so he threw it away and cracked open another. It tasted about as good as the first leg had the previous day, so he ate the whole thing and waited. He didn't get sick and considered himself incredibly lucky.

On the morning of the tenth day since Jacques woke up in the CSU, he had starch, protein, fruit, and his emergency kit was intact. There were a dozen hirachnoid legs and four bitterwood tree fruits in his basket. He had painstakingly depilated a hirachnoid pelt and sewn it into another bag. He'd constructed a back frame from flute plant stalks and green twine to carry things in. He laughed at himself; he was becoming a stone age man of substance.

He had now stayed at the same campsite for three days. It had a running brook, in which he'd bathed without incident–if there were local parasites, they didn't recognize him as food. He had been through a local rain shower, kind of a warm gently descending mist with the lightest of breezes that nevertheless had managed to soak everything. He had taken to going around naked—less itching, less sweating, and less wear and tear on an emergency suit he might need later.

He had fire, though it had taken hours of experiment with a green twine bow and stick to get something going. Then he had a hell of a time containing it—the Resolution had found a planet with perhaps an Earthlike percentage of oxygen in its atmosphere, but the pressure here must be something like three or four atmospheres—so the partial pressure of the combustion-supporting gas was that much higher as well. He glanced around him at widely spaced trees, the largest ones being succulent bitterwood, or chitin-barked blackwood. No mystery there. It turned out that tanglegrass ignited easily and dried bitterwood charcoal would glow for days. He was beginning to feel like an old hand.

He estimated that he now only needed to spend only about a quarter of his waking time hunting and gathering and could spend the rest doing something else. What should that be? Did he have enough to do the trek back into the crater? It might mean someone else's life, though he considered that possibility faint. Another thought was of salvaging his CSU. If he could rig up some kind of power source, he might get it partially functioning again. From the rim, he could study more of the puzzling geography of this world, and maybe see some stars long enough to orient it in space. He could do such projects later; for now, he had to focus on a rescue effort.

Okay, he thought, back to the rim. He left a scratched rock plaque by his fire pit:

Deliverance Creek Camp
First Human Settlement
Jacques Song
Day 7-10

He frowned; he was into double digits now.

There was another trail across the creek; he had seen kangasaurs of various types going by on it. Why did they go up to the rim? he wondered. Well, he would have plenty of time later to study such matters. He spent the rest of the day trapping and gathering, then set off the next morning.

Upward with a full kit was still no stress whatsoever in the low gravity and hyperbaric oxygen. Eventually, he thought, he might be able to build an aircraft. Even a small wing area would support a lot of mass here.

He was lost deep in thought when a three-meter kangasaur attacked. He heard it coming and managed to turn and ward off the kick with his staff more by instinct than reason. "Where in the blue sky did you come from!" he yelled in surprise as he swatted another kick with his staff and backed away. His Earth gravity-bred strength, the quickness of his reactions, and the extension of his reach with the staff seemed to confuse the would-be predator, and for a moment, the two bipeds froze, eying each other warily, the beaked head of the kangasaur bobbing back and forth.

Sensing hesitation, Jacques Song, Killer Ape, roared as loudly and fiercely as he could manage and advanced on the confused beast, whipping his staff back and forth. Being hollow, it made a frightening moan in the dense air. The kangasaur jumped back, turned and began running away up the path.

Jacques stood there laughing, naked, sweaty and exhilarated. But as he turned to march back up the trail, he heard a much larger crunch. The kangasaur had returned with a pair of much larger ones, probably six meters tall, behind him. Unable to think of anything else to do immediately, Jacques swung his staff again. The smaller one immediately jumped back behind the large ones. After a heart-stopping five or six seconds the larger one jumped, its clawed foot–almost a meter across–looking to come right down on Jacques.

On Earth, he would have been dead meat, but it took much longer for things to happen here. Jacques stepped aside, then jumped himself as high as he could. The huge kangasaur's head followed the leaping human with an open beak. In midair, Jacques whipped his staff across the skull of the monster. There was a cracking splintering sound and it wasn't from Jacques' staff. The monster squealed in an incongruously high pitched voice and put its head between its front forelimbs.

"Sorry, I may have overreacted," Jacques said to it, in the humor of relief, as he sprinted up the trail away from the trio. It was the first time he had tried to run quickly since he'd arrived, and he found he had to carefully control his stride to keep from bouncing too high and losing speed to air resistance. The kangasaurs didn't pursue him, though, and he stopped after a few hundred meters.

"I may regret this," he told himself, but unable to control his curiosity, he retraced his steps. The small kangasaur family was clustered around the wounded animal, the other two nudging it with their beaks as it continued to hold its head in its forelimbs. A very bright red fluid, apparently blood, had wetted its foreclaws and limbs. Eventually, it stood up, and tried to walk, but blundered into a nearby tree. In an entirely human gesture, the smaller one reached for the forelimb of its wounded mother or father–Jacques thought of them as a family–and led it away from the forest and back down the path the way it had come. The other large one stayed behind, looking back up the trail. Its eyes met Jacques'. Jacques whipped his staff around in a circle and it made the odd moaning sound. The kangasaur's head bobbed, looking up at Jacques and then back toward the rest of its family. Finally it turned and followed them down the trail.

Jacques exhaled and continued upward on the trail, much more alert now, walking softly, and looking up and down the trail at every turn. The era of carefree strolls in the park was over.

# CHAPTER 4
# REQUIEM FOR A MARTIAN

The trees began to shrink and the forest thin as he approached the rim. The sky became soft and hazy with mist. The sun overhead was red and faint to the point where Jacques could look right at it; indeed, through the haze it began to look like what some pre-astronautical artists had thought a red dwarf would look like from a planet. Upward. While his eyes were on the increasingly jagged path through the lava ahead of him, the light suddenly dimmed. Jacques looked up in time to see the last of some great, indistinct silhouette pass across the large red disk. He shivered despite the warmth of air, thinking about wing loading in a dense atmosphere under low gravity with plenty of oxygen. Something was up there. Something big.

He looked at the trees—cover was beginning to get scarce. He built a stone cairn and scratched a crude picture of a bat-like thing on a piece of smooth pahoehoe lava. This he put on the cairn just under the top stone. As he brushed his hands off, he noticed a piece of paper caught between two stones on the ground. It was such an ordinary piece of litter that he almost turned away without recognizing its implication.

He was not alone.

Excited, he lunged for the paper before it blew away. It turned out to be a page from an old-fashioned diary–something one might indeed take into one's CSU. The ink had smeared and faded, but he could read some of the entries:

*...daddy spanked me - not ready for church on time...*

*...went to Blu River concert with Fredrika, Gus, and Tsen...*

*...algebra is too hard!!!! maybe Gus will help me but I won't let daddy know...*

*...went to Solis Lacus Temple Sunday, really, really beautiful. I feel inspired...*

*...Fredrika's 14th birthday party really fun but sad. Her folks sold her to Will Tharsis so goodbye. I wonder who daddy will sell me to? Just one more year–I don't want to go. I'm afraid.*

Feeling like a voyeur, Jacques didn't read any more. These were scenes from a New Reformationist childhood on Mars–and an understandable excuse to volunteer for a century-long expedition to liberate a people suffering from theocratic tyranny. Was this just a page come loose or had something bad happened? Jacques looked around for clues–but the page might have blown from anywhere by now.

The writer was probably female, he thought. Who? There was someone called Ascendant Chryse, a biotechnician in the third squad; she wasn't necessarily the only Martian farm girl on the expedition, though–just one whose name was memorable. She was tall and reserved, with long straight hair, and had been a bit of a loner. But something had burned in her eyes and she'd worn her jumper open low enough to show cleavage.

He put the diary page in his breast pocket. In the best of all possible worlds, he would have a chance to return it. Adam and Eve scenarios sprang unbidden in his mind.

He reached the rim before sunset. It was too hazy to watch the sun go down; things simply got dark with their usual suddenness. In the fading light, he managed to find a lava tube with a view to the East across the caldera and set up his bivouac on a hollow filled with soft volcanic sand.

He woke when it was still dark. Had he heard a noise? He listened carefully, but everything was silent now. He pulled the boots from his shipsuit on and felt his way out to relieve himself. Outside, he was greeted by one of the clearest and steadiest skies he had ever seen.

The air was dead still and only the faintest stars shimmered ever so slightly.

To the north, rising plumes of steam lit by a faint red glow reminded him that he was on the rim of an active volcano.

The star patterns were unfamiliar and were dominated by a brilliant red star so bright that it cast a shadow and degraded his night vision. He had to block it with his hand to see the Milky Way. But a group of second magnitude stars caught his attention; it looked like Orion's belt. With a start, he realized that it could indeed be Orion's belt, but viewed from hundreds of light years further away, and, if the still brilliant red and blue stars above and below it were Betelgeuse and Rigel, somewhat off to the side. Ophiuchus lay near Scorpius; Orion hunted on the opposite side of Earth's sky. So the brilliant red star to its right could be Antares; if so, they had passed a few light years beyond the heart of the Scorpion. With a bit of searching, he found what he thought were the Pleiades. Somewhere in the direction he was looking would be Sol, maybe a hundred times dimmer than the dimmest star he could see. The compact binoculars in his emergency kit required power, of course.

He would build a telescope to see Sol, some day. He could grind and polish an obsidian mirror, silver it somehow, and use the lenses from the binoculars as an eyepiece. If he couldn't get home again, he vowed he would at least see home again.

A brisk wind hit him from behind and a great dark void filled the sky where brilliant stars had been moments ago. Some primordial instinct seized him and he threw himself down to the lava as something he couldn't see went *whoosh-clunk!* above him. The stars reappeared as the black shadow flew off to the east. It was some kind of bird or bat, but the size of a large aircraft—a megabat. With the Milky Way behind it, he could see it bank and began to return. Terrified, he scrambled on all fours back to his lava tube. There was an audible, hollow thump-crunch outside as if a giant had jumped down on the lava field.

Jacques fumbled for his staff and basket and moved further into the lava tube, glad that he had chosen a small one. Loud scraping sounds commenced at the tube entrance, followed by the thumps of falling rock. Eventually they stopped, but Jacques stayed awake sitting on his haunches and gripping his staff the rest of the night.

When it got light enough to see he tended the variety of scrapes and scratches he'd gotten from blundering around blind and naked in the sharp lava field. Then noting the monster's excavation efforts hadn't shortened the tube significantly, he lay down on his space blanket and slept.

When he woke, he gathered his things and cautiously poked his head out of the lava tube. The sun was high, peeking through occasional gaps between impossibly tall dark-bottomed clouds that were rapidly filling the sky.

He emerged and looked around—not a hundred meters to his left, sitting in a depression of lava sand, were three huge eggs; he recognized the mottled shells.

Did he risk the climb down to the lake? He hadn't seen anything on the way up; maybe the megabat only hunted at night. Was there any point? The megabat was another reason not to expect to find any other survivors. Or maybe it wasn't a threat at all and was only protecting its clutch. Supposing he risked a search, what would be the best way of doing it? Going along the rough lava ashore would be time-consuming and increase exposure to the megabats. But if he were on or in the water, he could dive to escape it—trusting that said dive didn't take him into the jaws of a parrot-beaked shark.

He could make a boat of some kind. A hollow blackwood log should float nicely enough if one could stop up the ends. Bitterwood pulp dried out to something like cork, so that might work. He could braid ropes of green twine. He headed back down the hill and established a working camp at a level where there were logs of about the right size, a running brook, and a lava tube cave just the right size for him and nothing bigger. He called it Forest Camp.

Two weeks later, on Day 25, on the first landing beach, he had assembled four blackwood logs, stopped and sealed, about thirty centimeters across and four meters long—as large as he could carry—along with a coil of three-centimeter-thick green twine rope, numerous flute plant shafts, and a pile of mature blackwood leaves. The next morning, he pondered whether to follow his plan and go for one more log, or just go with what he had. One more log would make the raft about 1.5 meters across instead of 1.2. He looked at the high waves and decided to do it.

By this time, the path was well traveled. Carrying a log on the way back, with an overnight stop at Rim Cave, would take a day and a half. But unburdened, he could do it in half a day, so he took off immediately, intending on arriving at Forest Camp by early evening.

As he approached the rim, he witnessed an astounding sight. A group of kangasaurs had gathered at the megabat nest and were apparently trying to break open one of the eggs.

Almost by instinct Jacques rushed toward them, waving his arms, hoping to scare them away and save the eggs from the kangasaurs and the kangasaurs from momma megabat. But the kangasaurs didn't scare and one of them started toward him. Jacques slowed and prepared to do battle with his staff. Then he saw a long scar on the head of one of the kangasaurs that stayed by the eggs. Could it be the same one he hit before? Jacques began to whip his staff around, creating the low moaning sound and approached slowly. The scarred kangasaur left the egg clutch and started heading downhill; the rest followed. The one that had come to challenge him looked back at the retreating group, looked a Jacques, then back at the retreating group and abruptly turned and bounded after them. Jacques was curious about how much damage the kangasaurs had done to the eggs, but decided discretion dictated that he *not* approach the nest.

Instead, he continued quickly along his trail to Forest Camp. A distant movement caught his eye. A huge megabat was coming in for a landing; though it must have been moving rather quickly, it was so large that even rapid movements took time. In this slow motion, it settled to the ground among the trees as if using some antigravity mechanism.

Jacques scolded himself about curiosity and went to take a look anyway, careful to stay in the cover of the trees. The megabat itself was an ugly chimera of familiar-seeming things; a bear's head with a parrot's beak on the body of a bat. On the ground it squatted on its hindquarters, balancing with a pair of clawed fingers that projected from halfway out on its wings. Its neck didn't seem long in proportion, but still could extend some distance from its body.

What it held nearly made him retch. It had pulled something out of the wreckage of a CSU, a bloated, white thing that nonetheless had recognizable arms and legs. The corpse fell in half as the megabat's beak lifted it, and the monster gulped the half it retained with a quick motion of its head. Then it went back down for the rest. Shuddering, Jacques hid behind a blackwood tree until the megabat lifted off with a single mighty beat of its huge wings and vanished into the gloomy, clouded sky.

He went forward to see what had happened. It turned out that the CSU was not badly damaged–the megabat only dented it in the process of biting off the flexidiamond canopy. The fall, he realized, would not have been so bad. Terminal velocity for something the size of a CSU in this dense atmosphere and low gravity would be a fraction of what it was on Earth–maybe less than ten meters per second, and even that may have been broken by the tree canopy.

The occupant had made a camp around the CSU, apparently hoping to be rescued. A crude table and chair sat beside the CSU, made of flute plant shafts lashed together with green twine.

There was a basket, not unlike his, with personal effects in it. The remains of a handwritten book remained open, several pages having come off. Fearing the worst, he compared the page he had been carrying with the book. It matched; the CSU had been that of Ascendant Chryse.

His nose told him that she had been dead for a while when the megabat found her. He nerved himself to look into the CSU. Her decayed head was mercifully turned away from him amidst the scattered, putrid gore left by the unfastidious megabat. He hoped the bacteria in her body would kill the thing. But probably not–parasites coevolve with their hosts.

The shadow of the caldera had moved over him by this time. He would have to get back to Forest Camp quickly–the megabats, apparently, were already about their appointed rounds. He looked around for her emergency kit items, finding the bag, space blankets, canteen–everything but the solar array and wrist comp. Was the array working? It had to be around somewhere. He couldn't find it, however.

He was about to leave when he remembered the CSU memory; it might have a more complete record than his own. He found the access panel and the right side and, hopefully, turned the power on. The tiny engineering status screen display lit up immediately–her CSU had probably used much less power than his after landing. For one thing, it wouldn't have needed to make air.

But the external intake status was "off." That didn't make sense to him. With the power off and the canopy shut, and the vents closed, she would have suffocated. Had she simply given up hope and killed herself? That didn't make sense, but the evidence seemed to point that way.

Shadows were deepening. He pulled the systems control module out of the CSU and took it and the diary back with him to Forest Camp.

That night, in his lava tube by the light of glowing charcoal, he got to know Ascendant Chryse and her history. She would not, he thought, have killed herself expecting to go to heaven–as an adult, she had utterly rejected the mythology she'd been taught by the people who had abused her childhood. She had become a conforming Anglican, though with private doubts. She hated the New Reformation. The last pages of her diary flamed with her determination.

He wouldn't be able to play back her CSU's record of the *Resolution's* journey until he found another undamaged CSU, but in the last pages of her diary, she vowed to "...get revenge for the sabotage that diverted *Resolution* from 36 Ophiuchi." There was no despair in this writing, or anything like it.

Needing some closure, he tore out an empty page of Ascendant's diary after her last entry. Some of the cells of her body would be on that, along with her fingerprints. Also, it represented her future, the unwritten pages of a life that might have extended to the end of time itself. Gone now. He took the page and lit it afire from his charcoal lamp. Its brilliance filled his small cave for a few seconds, then flickered out.

He sang Heinlein's *Green Hills of Earth* softly and went to sleep with tears in his eyes and an unanswered question in his mind.

Sabotage required a saboteur. Who? It would have been a suicide mission... or maybe not. He was alive, after all.

# CHAPTER 5
# BEYOND SURVIVAL

He arrived at Rim Camp in early evening. Days had become noticeably warmer and longer since he'd emerged, but the sun still rose at nearly the same place on the horizon each day. At least it did as far as he could tell without stopping to build some kind of a Stonehenge to measure it. The change must be due to orbital eccentricity, he thought. He stuck his thumb out at arm's length to cover less of the sun.

Two days later, after some thought and exploration, Jacques assembled the log raft *Resolution II* on a black sand beach three hundred meters clockwise from where he originally came ashore. The area had a small protected cove, an unusual two-story lava tube cave, and a shoreline of about thirty meters or so of deep black sand. There, he had room to lay the five corked blackwood logs parallel and rope them together with green twine. On top of the logs, he laid out a dozen smaller blackwood branches at right angles, and tied them down with a lot of green twine. On top of the middle three of those, he lashed a platform of some thirty flute plant shafts, about three meters long and 1.5 meters wide, each jammed into its own hole in a blackwood log, fore and aft. On top of this, he secured a block of dried bitterwood to serve as a seat. Three long, reasonably straight blackwood branches served as oars—one was a spare.

He launched *Resolution II* on day 30. It worked reasonably well in the relatively calm waters of the cove, but tipped so much in the higher waves of the lake that he had great difficulty staying on his seat. He rowed back to the beach and made another trip to the forest for more green twine and provisions.

Finally, on day 33, having made a green twine seat belt with a whittled buckle, he felt ready for open water. While the waves were high and steep, they moved slowly and he was able to get into a rhythm of waves and oars that let him progress at maybe two meters a second without too much effort.

He wore his emergency suit—mainly for the clear visor that let him see well underwater. Every hundred yards or so, he would unstrap, dive, and look for a CSU. About a quarter of the way around the lake, he found one.

The CSU was perhaps at half the depth of his and still functional. Its occupant was a man of medium height, a deep tan, and straight black hair. Jacques didn't recognize him. He tied a line to the CSU and opened its panel to start the revival process. Then he went back to the raft to catch a breath and wait. After what he judged to be about twenty minutes, he dove again. The man seemed about as startled to see him as Jacques had been to see the parrot-beaked shark—a thought that made Jacques glance around nervously.

By placing his inflated hood right against the CSU, Jacques was able to tell the man what to do, and soon the two of them were together on the raft.

"What happened?!" was the first thing the man said after pulling his hood off. "My CSU couldn't tell me anything. It was barely functional." He was a wiry, dark man and spoke with what Jacques thought was a slight British or Australian accent.

Jacques shook his head. "The same thing for me. I'm not at all certain, but apparently the *Resolution* could not, or was not allowed to, decelerate at 36 Ophiuchi and its AI or its crew or both did the best they could to find this place and dump the CSUs here. So far, I've found one who didn't make it, and you."

"Submahn Roy," he said and offered a hand. "From Bengal. Just call me Soob. I was a park ranger and safari leader. I was going to have a hand at occupation logistics."

Jacques gave Soob the basics of his lonely odyssey. "I have Chryse's CSU control module; it may have more data, but I need another CSU to play it. We might try to raise yours."

"I'm not good for much physically, right now. But as soon as I am, we should look for others."

Jacques nodded. Time was running out on the underwater CSUs, and more people would make the job easier. He dove to recover his line and mark Soob's CSU with a green twine-tethered blackwood buoy, then they rowed back to the beach.

Soob recovered as rapidly as Jacques in hyperbaric oxygen, and they were able to set out again the next day to look for others. The first CSU they found was occupied by Lieutenant Collette Obota, an African woman from the Congo. She was a member of the expedition's twenty-person police force–tiny, but any actual fighting would have been done by robots under human direction. A tall, personable, lady with a big grin, Jacques had not met her before, but liked her instantly.

The occupant of the next CSU they found had clearly expired some time ago. The same for the next two. But the fourth was different. Its occupant looked to be of Asian ancestry and was still in hibernation. Jacques started the revival process from the access panel, and soon the occupant was aboard the raft. He introduced himself as Yu Song-Il, a psychiatrist, who had been born on Hanguk'i Habitat in the Proxima belt. Almost two hundred years old biologically, he greeted his new circumstances with the joy of discovery.

Not long after they pulled him aboard, it began to rain in huge cold drops that reminded Jacques of water balloons. They had to struggle to row against a gentle, but surprisingly insistent, wind and monster waves to get back to their beach. Green twine lashings began to fray and snap as the *Resolution II* flexed alarmingly.

A huge wave broke Jacques' basket open and its precious cargo of emergency kits and food spilled aft. Unhesitatingly, Collette dove after them.

For a second, Jacques froze, then shouted. "Soob, Doc Yu, take the oars and try to keep us steady." Then he scrambled after the remaining supplies on all fours as the raft pitched up and down. His hand clamped on a coil of nanotube line before it had a chance to slither overboard. He wrapped this around the broken basket several times in a crude repair. Reluctantly, he cut that part off with the multitool, tied the end around several deck boards and tied the other end to a loop on his emergency suit. Then he dove into the water to look for Collette. It had all taken several minutes and she was nowhere to be seen.

"Collette!" he screamed at the top of a wave. Three times he screamed.

"Over here!" he heard at last. He swam toward the sound.

It became difficult to breathe as the drops became more and more dense. It was impossible to avoid inhaling water, and he coughed as he struggled. He lost his direction. There was nothing to do but tread water and call again.

Something brushed against his foot. Instinctively, he kicked. Suddenly he felt a strong tug on his boot and a sharp pain. Ducking underwater, he saw that a three-meter parrot-beaked fish had clamped its jaws around his foot. Unable to pierce the emergency suit, it was still exerting crushing force. In desperation, he bent double and punched it in the eye with all the strength his full-gravity muscles could manage.

No effect.

Trying to calm himself, he got his multitool out, opened the blade, and sank it deep into the fish's skull. Nothing. Lungs burning, he slashed behind its head, once twice.

On the third cut, it released him and swam erratically away. Jacques pushed himself to the surface.

"Over here!" he heard. Not twenty meters to his right, Collette was treading water with two emergency kits in her arms. With arms that felt like lead, he stroked over to her. With Collette gripping him with her legs, she pulled them both back to the raft.

It held together, barely, for the immeasurable time it took to get back to the cove. When they arrived, Jacques could see that the wave line of the lake shore had already advanced almost a meter. Together, they dragged the raft as far up onto the shore as they could, tied it to a stick they wedged into a small lava tube and carried what was left of their supplies into the Lava cave. They had lost all the indigenous food, but only one bag of emergency gear.

Exhausted, they spent the entire next day in the cave, consuming nutrition bars and creating small private areas with shards of fallen pahoehoe lava cleared from the floor. The raindrops hitting the top of their cave sounded like distant, muffled drums. At one place, water dripped down from the roof of the lava tube. They "corked" a segment of hollow blackwood log left over from the *Resolution II's* construction, a volume of about half a cubic meter, to place beneath it.

Jacques nursed his swollen foot and recounted his adventures as the storm subsided. He also made another plaque:

New Landing, Day 35
Great storm. Rescued–

Below he laboriously scratched in the full names of his party.

Rainwater, seeping in, filled a large sandy-bottomed depression in the lower part of the cave, and they bathed in shifts. Then they washed their shipsuits and hung them to dry.

Jacques arose before the others to watch the sun rise the next day. While he was happy to have achieved his goal in rescuing other survivors, he had grown used to being alone and not entirely unhappy with it. In the morning light, he found the shore almost lapping at their cave entrance and the remains of the *Resolution II* bobbing in the still-disturbed lake at the end of its tether. He found a secure place above the cave entrance to place his plaque and went back in to wake the others.

There was, he realized a decision to make. Most of the camp outside the lava tube had been washed away. The raft was in no shape to set out again, but every day, every hour, of delay meant that someone might die who might otherwise be saved. Alone, Jacques would have gone back to forest camp for more supplies. Now, with others present who might question his judgment, he hesitated.

Collette stepped smoothly into the silence with a clear, bell-like voice. "Here we are, four naked savages at the mercy of storms and hungry monsters with dreams of climbing back to starflight. Well, what should we do, Jacques?" Collette asked. "You know this place better than we do."

Jacques looked around at them, uncertain.

"What would you do if we weren't here?" Doc Yu asked.

Jacques told him.

"Ah." Yu smiled. "And how does our being here change that?"

Jacques shrugged. His situation had suddenly moved from straightforward survival to something involving leadership and perhaps even politics. He was not comfortable with that.

"With all of us working together, we should be able to do it faster," Soob interjected. "We can hunt more, and carry more. I think we should add another log to the raft, and some more cross bracing."

Jacques looked around him. Heads nodded. A consensus seemed to be forming. "Very well. Let us pack our things and go. We should be able to make Rim Cave by sunset if we leave now." The sun, he reflected, seemed to be larger, warmer and up longer than when he first revived. But he had no way of measuring it.

About halfway up the caldera wall, Jacques saw a dark shape against a towering white cloud.

"Everyone, look up, about thirty degrees left of the trail. That's a megabat."

"It looks as big as an airliner," Collette said. "Do you think it's the one that ate Ascendant?"

"I've only seen one at a time, but I can't imagine there's only one in the whole ecosystem. I think they prefer feeding at night; probably see well into the infrared."

"The one that ate Ascendant," she replied calmly, "was one that found something to eat in the daytime."

Jacques nodded nervously and increased his pace as they all took turns watching the sky.

They reached Rim Cave at sunset and nervously worked to expand its sleeping area well into twilight. The soft *whummm, whummm* of huge wings were heard in the night, but no long beak attempted the entrance this time.

As dawn broke, Collette and Jacques found themselves together outside the cave mouth.

"An early riser, too, I see," she said.

"And one with a French given name, too. This seems auspicious." Jacques smiled.

"It's my mother's name. My parents met in Kindu, centuries ago now," Collette said. "It dates from the Belgian colonial period."

"My great grandmother was a French diplomat in Papua New Guinea," Jacques replied. "My great grandfather was a Hong Kong businessman. They settled there, in the high mountains. Someone in each of the last four generations has had a French given name."

At Forest Camp, hunting and gathering was problematic. There were few bitterwood tree fruits to be found, and those seemed well past their prime. Hirachnoids had grown scarce as well and for the first time, Jacques failed to see a kangasaur.

That night in the lava tube, Soob was worried. "It is very difficult to be sure, but we have found in one day somewhat less than is needed to sustain us for three—even supposing that we are not missing crucial trace nutrients. We need another food source. What else have you tried?"

Jacques shook his head. "My priority has been the rescue of other crew members. After finding enough to keep me going, I focused on that and did not take additional chances."

"I see."

"Did the bitterwood pulp wood actually make you sick?" Doc Yu asked.

Jacques laughed. "I didn't try very much."

"The molecules that cause the bitterness may be more fragile than the molecules of nourishment. I suggest we try cooking it. What about tanglegrass?"

"I haven't tried that at all," Jacques answered. Then he remembered what he'd seen when he'd caught his foot in some and pulled it out of loose earth. "It has a thick white root, however."

And so the conversation went. By mid-morning the next day, they had determined that bitterwood pulp was indigestible, regardless of what one did to it. Tanglegrass root was too hard to eat raw, but could be pounded into a paste that didn't make anyone sick; whether it was nourishing would have to be determined later.

But the big surprise, in Jacques mind, was flute plant fronds. Boiled, they proved almost indistinguishable from spinach. Young flute plant shoots also proved edible when boiled soft enough to chew.

They set out for Rim Cave by noon with a corked blackwood log and forty person-days worth of provisions. Soob and Doc Yu carried the log, packed with the supplies, while Collette and

Jacques headed over to Ascendant's CSU to see if there was anything else to salvage.

Jacques attacked the area behind the access panel with his multitool. Wires, connectors, optical fibers, braces, components—anything he could pull out quickly went into their emergency kit bags. In the main compartment, the smell had gone and Ascendant's skull lay, face still away, completely clean.

"She had beautiful bones," Collette said. "I wonder what cleaned them?"

"I don't know," he said. "Why?"

She smiled at him. "Protein." Then she laughed at his reaction. "There are only a few ways to do carbon-based life, and what we find here, like about 45% of what we find anywhere, must do it our way. If they can eat us, we might be able to eat them."

"We need to be on our way," Jacques said, recovering his equilibrium. "The sun is about halfway down."

As they strode up the fairly well-worn path toward Rim Cave and the tree-bearers, Jacques contemplated the path of their sun. It seemed to be setting in the same place, yet days seemed to be getting longer and hotter. The planet's orbit must be eccentric, he thought. How close to its sun would it get?

Lost in thought, he was utterly and totally surprised when one of the most bizarre apparitions he had ever seen in his life loomed in front of him, held up a hand and said, "Well, praise the Lord! Jack's Song, I presume?"

# CHAPTER 6
# COMMUNITY

It was a large ruddy-faced man dressed in a kind of cave-man get up–an animal skin of some kind wrapped around his waist and over a shoulder. He had a large bag made of the same skin slung over his shoulder and a large flute plant staff with the fronds still attached.

"That's me," Jacques said. "But how did you know? What do you call yourself?"

"Gabe Eddie." He stuck out a hand which Jacques shook. "Just call me Gabe. I was a psyche warfare troop on the *Resolution*. I'm from New Jerusalem. I've been following your trails for days now–all those cairns and markers, with your name on several."

"Of course," Jacques said.

"We need to catch up with the rest of our party," Collette said. "We have a camp on the rim in a Lava tube, which we should be in before the megabats come out."

"Jacques, you don't mind me joining your party, do you? My dragon hole's a little further south on the rim than yours."

"Agreed, but we should start walking," Jacques said, starting to pace up the trail. "My colleague is Lieutenant Collette Obota, of the expeditionary police."

A transient frown passed Eddie's face. "That's long ago and far away, now."

"Nonetheless, that is our governing authority. Anyway, we all live forever now. Empress Marie may still rule—and our laws as well."

Gabe's expression resolved itself into a smile and a nod as he tagged along. "Well, maybe. But your gal's prettier than the Empress is, though a bit underdressed."

Collette laughed. "But very comfortable. How do you put up with that... skin?"

"Smoked, scraped, soaked, scraped, and soaked. Rendered some fat to oil and soften it."

"Really?" Collette sounded skeptical. "Gabe, do you know more about how we got here?"

"More than what?" There was a hint of wariness in this answer of a question with a question.

"None of our CSUs seem to have a full record of what happened at 36 Ophiuchi, except that the homing lasers failed. *Resolution* didn't stop there and ended up here."

"Mem'ry triage," Gabe said, quickly. "Takes power to correct and refresh memory—when the CSUs get low, they skip whatever ain't immediately needed. I'd guess we all been here a while. Wakin' someone up alone at the bottom of the sea is kind of the last resort."

The power needed to refresh memory was trivial, but Jacques didn't want to start out on Eddie's wrong side. He simply said, "That's interesting. Do you have any ideas, Collette?"

"Those who crashed on land may have used more power for cooling than those of us deep in the lake needed for oxygen," she said. "That's why there's still hope to rescue some more."

"You kill a dinoroo, yet Jacques?" Gabe asked

"Dinoroo? There is an animal I call a kangasaur. That's a bipedal hopper about six meters tall as an adult, pretty much hairless."

"That's a dinoroo!"

"I almost killed one by hitting it in the head when it came at me. They've left me alone since—I wonder if they aren't able to communicate the danger to each other?"

"Wouldn't know. I got me a whole family of 'em with a spear thrower, though—great meat and useful skins. Almost like the Lord put 'em there for us. Haven't seen many around lately, though."

"Me neither," Jacques answered. "I suspect something seasonal." He saw movement on the path ahead of them. "There's Soob and Doc!" During the conversation, they'd caught up with the tree bearers. Collette gave her emergency bag to Jacques and rushed forward to help.

With three people carrying the blackwood log, they were able to arrive at Rim Cave well before sunset. Excited by the new arrival, they talked well into the night, comparing notes. Gabe told of hunting at night, from blinds, and had observed a list of critters Jacques hadn't seen, including what he called a "roachrunner," a hairy beetle-like thing that went after any meat left out for more than an hour.

"You wouldn't believe how they fly," he said. "No sound at all. They just float up. I swatted one once; it kind of popped."

For his part, Gabe was surprised that the legs of "spinyballs," as he called the hirachnoids, were edible. Jacques offered him one of the last remaining ones, but Gabe turned it down. "Got my own meat," he said.

∞◊∞

The next morning Jacques and Collette got up to watch the sunrise. It was even bigger and redder near the horizon.

"I don't believe this character," Collette said. "New Jerusalem?"

Jacques shook his head. "New Jerusalem is a big Baptist space colony at the Earth-Sun L4 point. We had a lot of old-line Christians among the volunteers. From our point of view, it may seem like a family fight, but nobody was more ready to go after this New Reformation fringe group than the Old Reformation."

Collette nodded. "I get the picture. Well, he's going to need to realize this isn't New Jerusalem, and it isn't going to be."

"We're all in this together now," Jacques said.

"Watch," Collette said. "Just watch."

∞◇∞

The walk from the rim down to the beach only took an hour in the relatively cool morning. The water had receded since the storm and the *Resolution II* was laid out on the sand, its five logs barely held together—mostly by the remaining lashings of its deck braces. The cargo basket was pretty much gone, but they'd brought the makings of another. With five people working, the expanded raft was shipshape again before sunset.

At daybreak the four men lifted the raft and carried it to the water. "I'm not much of a swimmer, so you three go on," Gabe said. "I'll hold down the fort here."

At that point, Collette carried a supply basket down to the raft and handed it up to Doc. She and Jacques pushed the back end of the raft off the sand, jumped on, and waved goodbye to Gabe. Gabe stood on the shore alone, dressed in his Robinson Crusoe costume, open-mouthed, then seemed to recover himself and returned their waves.

It was very hot on the lake and surprisingly still. As they rowed, they had time to talk.

"It is too bad we do not have any working electronics," Doc said.

Jacques nodded. "Given a thousand years with no maintenance, it's not that surprising. Even my photovoltaic unit didn't work."

"You thought it might?" Collette said. "Maybe we should try mine."

Focused on the rescue effort, they had been too busy during daylight hours to perform any such experiments. Collette got her emergency kit and they spread the array on the slightly rolling deck and plugged it into the kit's wrist comp. Nothing happened. They tried Jacques'. It stayed dark. Then they tried Soob's. The comp screen glowed. Jacques felt a surge of relief. Maybe they wouldn't have to reinvent everything.

"Time?" Soob said. But the screen stayed blank. The device refused to recognize any commands.

"We have power," Jacques said at last. "And five wrist comps. When we get back, maybe I can make a working one using pieces of all five."

"People!" Doc shouted. "Below us, a CSU!"

Jacques scrambled over to Doc's side and looked down—it was deep, maybe as deep as his had been. That was hopeful.

Collette donned her emergency suit. By consensus, she and Jacques were the best swimmers. Soob tossed overboard green twine line weighted by a net full of rock to serve as an anchor and communication line. After first sticking their heads in the water to look for parrot-beaked sharks, they dove.

They came up with Edith Lu. She had spent a day trying to get her damaged CSU to release its canopy—which Jacques managed in seconds from the controls under its access panel. Once on deck, she threw her arms around Jacques and sobbed.

By sunset, they had completed their circumnavigation of the lake and counted two new companions and four non-survivors. Besides Edith Lu, they found social engineer Maria Lopes. Despite being in shallow water, Lopes' CSU seemed to be in the best shape, and they took careful note of its location for potential future salvage.

The *Resolution II* rowed out the next two days, crisscrossing the lake, but no more CSUs were found. Submahn, however, operating on the hunch that behavioral evolution may have had some parallels, made a trap and snared a two-meter parrot-beaked shark. He also caught a previously unseen flat, eel-like critter and what looked to be a lacustrine version of a hirachnoid. The shark proved delectable.

When they returned, they had three more mouths to help eat it.

Leo Suretta, a weapons engineer, had left his CSU-based campsite in the forest and, like Gabe, had followed Jacques' cairns to New Landing. A small, dark man with straight black hair, he had little to say. Evgenie Malenkov, a tall, blond biologist from Coriolis, Luna, an expert in artificial ecologies, had wandered in from a CSU landfall the other side of the mountain with Arroya Montez, a diminutive cyberneticist of striking beauty, who stayed very close to Evgenie and spoke very little.

Maria Lopes was another matter entirely. A talkative forester from a Portuguese family, she almost immediately started a theological debate with Evgenie, who Jacques took to be Reformed Orthodox, or something of the sort. Lopes was Roman Catholic.

Edith Lu nodded her head to the theological discussion. "Ascendant would have loved that."

"You knew her?" Jacques asked.

"We were physical skills training partners. She was convinced the Anglican communion had found its way to a world view that was both Christian and consistent with 'the book of nature,' as she called it. She liked to quote Bacon."

"Are you part of any belief system?" Jacques asked. He'd been raised Buddhist, himself, but had given it up, unwilling to swallow the notion of rebirth, and unwilling to ignore it.

Edith shook her head, "As far as I can tell, what you see is what you get. My people have some wonderful old rituals that are fun to reenact, as long as you take them allegorically, and not too seriously at that. I suppose I'm Confucian, in a way. I like traditions, and feel comfort in them, but I don't ascribe magical powers to them."

At dusk, they retreated to the cave, created more rooms, and then slept as people got tired. Sometime in the night, Edith found her way to Jacques' "room" and nestled in beside him.

"Are you sure this is wise?" he asked.

"You're the only one I know," she said. "Just hold me. Please don't send me away."

Jacques didn't. They'd had one night together while at the academy, a very sweet but unexciting experience for him. While he was fond of Edith in a brotherly way, he hadn't seen her as a partner; they were both too reticent. In a good pairing, he thought, people's natures would be complementary, filling in each other's weaknesses and abating each other's enthusiasms. He dreamed of a strong partner, to compensate for his own hesitation and diffidence.

On day 37, the CSUs of Helen Gorgos and Dominic Oporto were found in deep water not far north of New Landing. Helen, a physicist, struck Jacques as a gentle, thoughtful lady while Dominic was short, bright, and bubbly.

After he'd recovered from his ascent from his CSU, and been apprised of the situation, Dominic announced that he was not giving up the mission. "I will return to 36 Ophiuchi!" he declared. "I do not care if 1000 years have passed. If things have not changed there, I will try to change them. That is what I left everything to do; so it is my life. It is my goal."

Jacques smiled at that. "Mine as well. If I have to rebuild civilization from the stone age up to do so, I will do it!"

∞◇∞

Finally, on day 39, they declared the rescue effort over. Of 200 CSUs on the *Resolution*, they had found a total of fifteen in the lake, six with live occupants. If there were others, elsewhere on this planet, they were beyond reach for now.

Gabe, who had some experience as a lay minister, led a memorial service at the lake shore. "We give up them up to God," he concluded, "and pray for His guidance as we take up the task of our own survival."

That night, they sat around a fire on the beach and talked about what they wanted to do. They might explore nomadically as a group or they might establish a settlement, then send out expeditions. Doc and Gabe, respectively, were the proponents of these positions.

"We have much to learn about this world," Doc argued. "And what we learn will affect what we do. We may find a much better place to start a city. It is very hot here, and this is an active volcano."

"But we gotta get our feet on the ground," Gabe countered, "start acting like human beings instead of a bunch of naked savages—not that I mind the scenery but the Lord made other plans for us long ago. Anyway, we need some place for explorers to come back to, if they run into trouble. If we all go exploring, it's a single point of failure. One disaster and, boom, we're all gone!"

"Smaller exploration parties would be easier," Soob said. "The surplus from the labors of the larger group can be concentrated to supply the exploration group and they can operate more efficiently, spending less time on provisioning."

"Yes, at some point," Doc said. "But it should be sited at a better place. There are four huge mountains around us. There will be some place on their slopes where the air and the temperature are more Earth-like."

"Maybe even above the altitude where the dragons fly," Collette added

Even she, Jacques thought, had started using Gabe's names for the life forms on this planet. He had, almost pointedly, refused to adopt Jacques' names, and it being a matter of no particular importance to anyone, others had began to adopt Gabe's nomenclature to avoid confusion.

The trouble was, on the issue at hand, Jacques agreed with Gabe. Small exploration parties made more sense. The dilemma was that to support that position would be to accede leadership to Gabe, which, for some reason, bothered him greatly. But he didn't want any kind of formal leadership position for himself. He might lead by example–not by argument or politics.

The discussion was winding down without his input, in favor of Gabe's. But many were waiting for him to say something. He was, after all, the first settler and the one who had organized their rescues. That should still count for something. What could he say?

"I am," he said, finally, "going to look for a better place for a colony on this world, and, eventually, a way to rejoin the rest of humanity. But I think it would be best to spend a few weeks in this area to recover more technology and learn more about where we are. Will it be a permanent settlement? That is a question for the future. If the volcano is active, it is not very active. The cave here at New Landing is large enough to house us for the foreseeable future. We can fish. We can try growing flute plant or even bitterwood. We can forage over the rim."

Doc looked at him thoughtfully. "I would choose days instead of weeks. Each day grows hotter, and to reach cooler high elevation we must first descend into even warmer low elevations and cross an ocean. Each day we wait will make that more difficult. But I must concede we are not ready to go today."

There were murmurs of assent around.

"Well then, it's settled," Gabe said. "Now let's start organizing who does what. Arroya, why don't you get busy with the other women and come up with some clothes for us. Evgenie and Doc, we need some more fish. I'll take Soob over the rim and get some more game for us. Jacques, why don't you go up to the rim and try to figure out where we are. Okay, everyone?"

Most agreed immediately. Jacques felt something important had happened to which he should object, but couldn't come up with a clear reason or argument against anything Gabe had proposed. Even spending time on clothes—if they went up a mountain to where it should be cool enough in the hot season, it might be too cool when the weather turned. So he stayed silent.

But Collette did not. "I will go to the rim with Jacques."

Gabe frowned momentarily, then said. "Let's go, everyone. God be with you."

Suretta and Arroya stood up, then stopped as everyone else sat still.

Jacques simply stood up and nodded. The others then rose and dispersed as well.

# CHAPTER 7
# FINDING A PLACE IN THE UNIVERSE

Jacques thought he would be glad for Collette's company; but what he got on the ascent to Rim Cave was a tongue lashing.

"You are letting him walk all over you," she concluded after rehashing the morning's events.

She was in the lead, and her flute plant staff sent shards of lava flying to punctuate every point she made. There was actually a kind of cadence to it; she was a natural orator, he decided. A pause in her monologue perhaps meant he should say something to defend himself.

"Really, Gabe was just making common sense observations about what needs to be done. I would have said very similar things."

"No, you would not have! You would not have relegated all the women to making clothes. You would not have ignored everything I said because I'm a woman. You would not slip in references to mythological deities every other time you open your mouth."

Jacques had to admit she was right. "Okay, he betrays his origins. That's probably the way it is on New Jerusalem. We'll straighten that out when we get back. I think Doc and Soob can keep him in check. Collette, he gave me just what I wanted; a chance to get away from politics and worrying about who does what and how everyone's going to eat. I have a couple of days now to stop and think about where we are, what we've got and how we can get back."

She stopped, turned, and walked into his arms. He held her for what seemed minutes.

Finally she said, softly, with her lips at his shoulder. "Jacques, I just do not want any part of what Mr. Gabe is dishing out. I am thinking I may just go away and start my own civilization. I would like to bring you along. Also, I have a mass murder and an individual murder to solve."

Jacques was still focused on recovering their technology base and getting out of here. "Perhaps that's a bit premature."

"Is it?"

"Collette, how can I tell? I'm an engineer. Give me an engineering problem and I fix it. I don't like fighting with people." He squeezed her a little tighter. "If there's a split, though, I think I'd rather be with you."

She kissed him. Then broke away. "We have to hurry up to Rim Cave before we become dragon meat."

"Megabat meat, Collette. Megabat."

"Hey, that's the spirit," she answered with a big grin, and seemed to fly away from him up the trail in big joyful leaps.

In the cave, he and Collette spent much of the night with their multitools, a nonfunctional wrist comp, and Ascendant's CSU control module. When he was done, he had the wrist comp's power jack twist-wired into the CSU control module. That was as far as he could go without sunlight. Morning would tell whether he got it right.

There was one more chore: he took a look outside. It was hazy, but he was pretty certain that he saw distorted Orion and Antares setting in the west. It wasn't a real measurement; he didn't even know if the time of night was comparable. But what he saw suggested that their little world had completed something like half an orbit in the intervening forty rotations or so.

He went back into the cave and lay down on the space blanket by Collette.

"Uh, hi." She yawned.

"Hi. Collette, I think I've got our orbit worked out, roughly. The period should be about 80 of our days here, which is about 90 Earth days–that kind of fits with red dwarf luminosity and our atmosphere. The sun is getting larger, maybe half again the size it was when I got here, so the orbit is fairly eccentric and we're probably getting closer–approaching periastron."

"Tell me all about it in the morning, okay?" She turned away and went to sleep.

∞◊∞

He was up for sunrise. He stood behind the cairn marking Rim Cave and noted where the sun rose behind the small hill to the east of him. He put another cairn there. By now, he was pretty sure this line wouldn't change, but even with this primitive setup, he should be able to confirm that lack of change to a fraction of a degree.

Collette came out with some warm tanglegrass root mash for his breakfast. Thanks to Gabe's predations on the kangasaur population, they had bone spoons to eat it with. He was scraping the bowl when Collette called his name and pointed to the sky.

"Jacques, what's *that*? A supernova?"

A star had appeared in the daylight sky, well above what Jacques had decided was the projected plane of their planet's orbit. It was far too bright to be a planet, he thought. Collette was probably right.

"If so, it's not near enough to affect us, I think."

"That's the first since 2148, and we're probably the first ones to see it."

Jacques laughed. "Too bad we cannot file a report. Well, let us see if I've succeeded in anything. This is going to take some time. While I'm at it, do you think you could draw a map from what you see from the high point on the ridge south of us?"

"On what?" Collette laughed. "Wait, I have an idea." She grabbed a shard of rock and scratched the deep ebony skin of her arm. The line stood out clearly, much lighter than the skin.

"Ouch," Jacques said. "That must hurt."

"Not much. Okay, see you later." She grinned and gave him a peck on the cheek, her left breast brushing his arm as she did so–but neither of them did anything to acknowledge this accidental intimacy.

"Be sure to be back well before nightfall; remember the megabats," Jacques said.

She nodded seriously and was off. As she left, Jacques, to his wonderment, found himself following her with his eyes. She was not what he had grown up with thinking was beautiful, particularly in her wide hips, curly hair and projecting face. Still she moved with an easy, powerful grace. But it was her mind, he thought–its quickness and spirit that attracted him and made her body seem beautiful.

He sighed. He would have to deal with this complication in his life later.

He spread out the array and carefully plugged it into the various wrist comps. Two of them lit up. With the multitool, he very carefully cut off the back of one that didn't work at all and one that lit. He worked painstakingly on this all day and when he was done, he had a working wrist comp, although it could not operate without the solar array.

With the sun setting, he hurried to the highest point of the rim and queried it for any other signals. It found three. One was another wrist comp, about the right direction and distance for New Landing, another was a CSU in the forest below and the third was apparently midway between the northernmost mountain and the easternmost mountain.

The wrist comp identified the third as the *Fortitude,* an atmospheric shuttle carried aboard the *Resolution.*

One survived! The wrist comp would never reach it at this range, but if he could get nearer...

It should be looking for them. The joy of seconds ago turned into a cold cramp in his stomach. Even if damaged in re-entry, it was self repairing and nuclear powered. Its AI should know where the CSUs went down and should be seeking them out, unless told not to.

*Someone may be playing games with us,* Jacques thought.

The wrist comp abruptly shut down as a shadow fell on Jacques and the array. His head spun away from the display to show a huge megabat gliding down toward him, beak open. He quickly looked around for his staff–in his excitement over getting a wrist comp working, he'd forgotten it. Nor had he thought to set up near a lava tube. The nearest trees were too far to reach before the megabat arrived.

He would make the thing work for its meal, anyway, he resolved, and started scrambling toward the trees, keeping his eyes open for sticks, loose chunks of lava, anything.

The megabat deviated from its course to follow him. About a hundred meters away now, its wings filled the sky.

Coming over a ridge, Jacques leaned far over, gathered his legs beneath him, and leaped toward the forest edge with as much strength as he could muster. Landing from his ersatz flight could be painful, he thought, but his speed had increased greatly. He couldn't spare a look back at the mega-bat, and resigned himself to the big crunch that would end it all. As he lost altitude, he brought his legs under him, and seeing a smooth spot, kicked off of that, staying airborne. His body, he realized, was acting as an airfoil in the thick atmosphere.

He risked a look back. The megabat had landed on its hind legs— the wing webs joined the legs far enough up the leg to let it do so, and was swinging its head back and forth between where Jacques was now and where he had been. Up close, the monster's sharp-edged beak was bigger than he was.

"Jacques!"

It was Collette. He turned his head to see her waving from a hundred meters or so down slope, on the edge of the trees, hurrying toward him.

"Jacques! Electric fields! You, me, the solar array!"

Damn! The monster must locate living prey by their electric potential, like a shark. If it thought his power supply was something to eat, the entire small community could be condemned to decades of struggle. Putting his feet in front of him, he managed a not-too-painful halt on a hillock of smooth lava.

Collette charged toward the monster waving her arms in the air. It turned its head away from the array, toward her.

They could probably out-jump the thing, he realized; their reactions and one-g muscles might be more than a match for it. He took a deep breath and strode toward it yelling "Here, here!"

It swept its head from Collette and lunged for him, incredibly quickly. Jacques' eyes found a large, somewhat dish-shaped fragment of lava and picked it up. With more instinct than deliberation or aim, he whipped the piece of lava toward the megabat's head, using the reaction from his throw to push him down to the ground much faster than the low gravity would take him. The piece of lava missed, but whether the flying rock had distracted the monster, or Jacques had simply ducked too fast for it to follow, the beak, snapped shut on empty air just centimeters above him.

There was only one place to avoid the next bite. Jacques jumped up, grabbed the neck of the megabat and pulled himself up behind its head, his hands gaining relatively easy purchase in its hairy pelt. The creature swung its head slowly side to side in confusion.

While trying to figure out what to do next, he felt a tap on his back.

"Fancy meeting you here!"

"Collette!" Jacques shouted. She'd jumped onto the creature as well.

"Hang on, I think we're going for a ride!" She grabbed handfuls of hair with both hands.

Behind them, vast wings rose and the creature gathered itself and uncoiled for a stately stretch into the air. The downstroke of the wings was hardly audible, but the whoosh of their backstroke was deafening.

They gained altitude like an airliner, and were soon soaring hundreds of meters above the lake and the landscape.

"It's a square!" Collette shouted.

Jacques looked around. Above the local cloud cover now, he could see the layout of the land as a whole for the first time. The four huge distant mountains, indeed, formed the corners of a huge square that looked almost geometrically perfect from their viewpoint. He shook his head; what this implied seemed impossible.

"It *looks* like a square," he shouted back to Collette.

In turning back to her, he'd shifted his grip and his hand found a firm ridge of flesh, almost hidden in the hairy pelt of the back of the megabat's head. As his hand grabbed it, the megabat screeched and turned its head to the right, banking right in the process.

Jacques shifted his grip to a less sensitive place and their course straightened out.

"I think I found its ears!" he said.

A sharp bank to the left in response to a tug indicated that they must be very sensitive organs.

While it was still light up where they were, a deep shadow had quickly covered the world below them, leaving the rim of the caldera for last.

"Let's see if you can make it go down!" Collette shouted.

Jacques nodded, instinctively pushing the rim of the megabat's ear down. Its head also went down, and they descended. By pushing, tugging and pulling he was able to get it to land in the fringe of the forest just below the rim of the caldera.

Collette laughed. "They're so big they don't have to be smart!"

With unspoken assent, both Jacques and Collette jumped for the branches of a passing blackwood tree. Just as well: on the ground, the megabat ducked its head to where its huge claws could reach its ears. Scratched, the megabat swung its head up, then, seeing them, moved quickly away, as a person might avoid a bumblebee. With a screech, it fled into the sky.

Jacques and Collette dropped from the trees, made their way up to the Rim, collected Jacques' apparatus, and made their way into the shelter of Rim Cave.

"Wow!" Collette said, "Just Wow!"

Whether from the adrenaline coursing through their veins, or the mutual realization that they'd come very close to losing each other, and that suddenly mattered, they were quickly in each other's arms. When they let go, Collette had a silly grin on her face, and Jacques realized his life had changed forever. However, from natural reticence, or prudence, he said nothing.

"It's a perfect square," Collette said. "As close as I could tell, this side of the world is a perfect square with a huge mountain on each corner, and it looks flat, too, except for this hump in the middle."

"The flatness may be an illusion; those mountains look like they stick way up out of the atmosphere."

"Uh-huh, but the gravitational field should still be radial, shouldn't it? So if the side of the world is flat, and gravity is radial, and atmosphere conforms to gravity, the edges would stick out." She made a ball of her fist and put her other hand flat on top of it.

Jacques tried to visualize it. If Collette's model were right, walking out to the edge of the square would feel like going increasingly uphill, even if the side was geometrically flat. He shook his head. "This is unbelievable. The compression under the corner mountains must be astronomical! I don't see how anything in nature could do that."

Collette looked him in the eye. "We're part of nature. We could do this, someday."

"Okay, it looks like an artifact."

"Where there's architecture, there may be architects!" Collette's eyes were bright with excitement.

"How old do you think this place is?"

"Don't know. With all the vulcanism, the oldest parts of the surface are maybe on the order of 100,000 years? I don't see any craters, except maybe on the mountain tops."

"The life forms have adapted to this gravity. Maybe evolved some. I'm thinking a time scale of at least a million years. Whoever is watching over this has a lot of staying power."

Collette frowned. "A century is still a long time to me. I wonder what it's like to know so much time. Maybe we'll get to ask them. Maybe we'll even get a ride home!"

Jacques laughed, "They're being pretty scarce."

That night, they made love for the first time, and afterwards, Jacques clung to Collette as if to the most precious thing in the universe to him. Then they went out and, cautiously staying close to the opening of Rim Cave, watched the stars.

"What are you looking at?" Collette asked.

"The bright yellow-white star over the North rim, about halfway up over the part of the rim lit by the north lava flow."

"Okay. It seems ordinary enough."

Jacques squeezed her hand. "Probably is. What's significant is that it hasn't moved from that position since forty days ago. I think it's our north pole star."

# CHAPTER 8
# TESTIMONY OF A GHOST

As soon as the sun cleared the rim of the caldera, Jacques plugged the solar array into Ascendant's CSU. The maintenance screen lit up instantly.

"CSU, what happened aboard the *Resolution*?"

The tiny speaker below the maintenance screen produced a tinny, minimally inflected voice. "I have no records of events before atmospheric entry. During atmospheric entry, there was structural failure of Sphere 4 and this CSU was ejected at 48 km altitude."

"The same thing as with all the other CSUs," Collette observed.

"I thought as much. Ascendant was a diarist. I'm hoping she did what I did. Do you have anything from after Ascendant's revival?" Jacques asked.

"I have a command trace and redundant copies of recorded messages."

Pay dirt! "Play the recording."

Ascendant Chryse had been awake for the approach to the 36 Ophiuchi system. She was well aware that a starship is at its most vulnerable during the months it took to decelerate from almost 90% of the speed of light, and as a passionate opponent of the New Reformation, if they were attacked, she had wanted to know about it and die fighting back.

Great precautions had been taken; for instance laying out the deceleration trails on the far side of 36 Ophiuchi from Sol, so that the reflection plume would be directed away from the star and shielded by the starships' bodies. Particles had been engineered to self-ionize at low temperatures. Additional rings had been added to better collimate and cool the exhaust plume.

According to Ascendant, surprise had been preserved; there was no indication whatsoever that their opponents had any idea that an invasion force was establishing itself in the 36 Ophiuchi system. But when it came time for the *Resolution* to decelerate, it had not done so.

Ascendant's voice was a mellow, throaty warble that the CSU's minimally functional speakers clearly did not do justice. "'Why aren't we decelerating?' I asked. It told me someone or something had removed key components of the homing beacon system. The particles that were supposed to be slowing us down were just blowing by us. I got out of the CSU to look."

"That took guts," Collette said.

Jacques nodded.

"Everyone else was suspended in CSU fluid," Ascendant's voice continued. "I couldn't find the beacon parts–the ship couldn't either, and there wasn't time to make new ones. But I did find someone else up and about. I kept hearing things. But whoever it was has blinded the ship to himself somehow. I told the ship to wake the Captain and it said his CSU was off line. I went to his room and turned it back on– just in time.

"We woke a couple of the other crew, and they implemented the "Ghost Ship" contingency plan, for if deceleration goes wrong. They've plotted a course that will pass near several stars near our line of flight–they'll look for habitable planets or moons as they get closer, but at best we'll be traveling for centuries. The ship put out the emergency magsail to slow down a little and change course a little. When it gets to the destination star, it passes through the star's solar wind and ultimately its atmosphere to lose most of its velocity, using the ship's magnetosphere as a reentry shield. If it survives all that and still needs to dump velocity, it will crash into the target planet's atmosphere, break apart and dump the CSUs. Those are pretty tough. If anyone is listening to this, I guess it must have worked. They think maybe ten percent of us will make it.

"The Captain risked a great deal by sending one low power encrypted message back to the base in the 36 Ophiuchi Oort cloud explaining what happened and pleading for a rescue if possible. But we aren't expecting rescue—any such attempt would reveal the base and endanger seventy plus other inbound starships. Against that, we're expendable, may the bastard that did this rot in hell! We all said our goodbyes and went to sleep."

"Including the saboteur," Collette said in a hushed when the record finished. "Ascendant made it through all that only to get murdered again! What sort of monster could do this?"

Jacques shrugged. "A fanatic willing to make the sacrifice? Or maybe one who thinks that some supernatural force would intervene."

In the silence that followed he heard something skitter down the slope above him. He turned his head in time to dodge a small stone heading for them, probably loosened by the warming day. A happenstance, certainly. But he looked around anyway. We are programmed to suspect some agency in everything that happens, he thought. Even when you know it's a random event, you look. Intervening gods, or devils, are easier to imagine than pointless chance.

Collette shook her head. "The saboteur probably wiped all the CSU records before going into cold sleep himself. He might have come across her camp while she was asleep or away, read her diary, then destroyed the incriminating pages and silenced her, not suspecting she'd left another record."

She looked at him, worry on her face. She clearly had devils of the non-supernatural kind on her mind. "Gabe. Does he know you have her CSU memory?"

Jacques went through the events of the past few days in his head. "I've not told anyone but Soob about Ascendant's CSU control module."

"We'll need to hide it," Collette said, "and bring Soob into our confidence."

"What about the shuttle?" Jacques asked.

"Assuming Gabe is the saboteur, it would be under his control, wouldn't it?"

Jacques thought carefully about that. "If the AI were intact, and convinced that Gabe, or whoever the saboteur is, had been responsible for human death, it might respond to another human authority. But someone who really knew what they were doing might have been able to degrade the AI just enough so that it wouldn't respond to higher function programming, but would still be flyable."

"So we're screwed?" Collette threw a small pebble at a nearby rock, clearly angry and not willing to submit to that fate.

"Maybe not. If the AI is intact, with Ascendant's record, I might gain control by argument. If not, it might not be able to stop me from getting physical access to the systems I would need to bring its higher functioning back on line. But there's a problem. The shuttle would certainly be programmed to report any attempt at access immediately. We'd have to be much closer to it–on site, preferably."

"Jacques, there's something else I think we should keep up our sleeve."

"Yes?"

"Our megabat ride–I'm not sure I want to do it again, but it's a transportation option maybe someone else shouldn't know we have."

Jacques nodded. "CSU, what's your power state?"

The display read twenty-three percent.

"That's up!" Collette exclaimed.

Jacques smiled. "But yes! We have some energy storage. CSU, what is the design width of your casing?"

It displayed 10.25 cm.

Jacques grinned. "We can now measure space and time accurately. We are about to leave the stone age!"

They plugged in the wrist comp, and got temperature and humidity–about 35 C and 20%. Atmospheric pressure was a whopping 3,123 millibars, and they were at least four kilometers above the lake.

By evening, they had determined with a pendulum that local gravity was 14.38% of Earth's. By the next morning, they had the local day pegged at 28.25 hours–significantly longer than Jacques had guessed. By the time they went to bed, they had a working hypotheses that their world was approximately moon sized; though somehow managing more extreme elevation differences. The orbital period was 91.48 Earth days, give or take a little–almost exactly 79 local days. It got substantially less insolation than Earth; it was hot where they were because of the deep, high pressure atmosphere–it would probably be well below freezing at the one bar level.

# CHAPTER 9
# SOCIAL ISSUES

They returned to the lakeshore about noon the next morning to find their small colony almost fully clothed. All the men except Doc Yu were wearing parrot beaked fish skin kilts. Edith and Maria were wearing muumuu-like tents. Helen Gorgos, the female exception, was talking to Doc, away from the others.

As soon as they came into camp, Edith ran up to Collette and handed her a dress.

Collette sighed and smiled at her. "Edith, I'm really comfortable the way I am."

Edith looked crestfallen and glanced back at Gabe and Leo, who were looking in their direction, then back at Collette. "I made it just for you," she said, plaintively. "Look, I even put your name on it." She held it out wide, with a hand on each shoulder.

There, just under the neckline, Jacques saw "Collette" embroidered in cursive letters on the parrot beaked fish skin with green twine.

"Will you just try it on for me? Please?"

Collette laughed, took the garment, and pulled it on over her head. She gave Edith a hug. "That must have taken a lot of work. I'm sure this will come in handy when we get in a colder place."

Edith beamed.

Gabe came up to them and thrust a piece of cloth at Jacques. "Well, looks like at least some of us are gettin' civilized."

Jacques took the cloth with a smile, but simply held it. Then he yelled, "Come on over everyone, I've got news."

"Hey..." Gabe said.

"Jacques," Leo said. "We appreciate what you've done, rescuing people and getting things started, but we've done some organizing while you've been away and..."

"Welcome back!" Doc said, holding out his hand.

"I was talking," Leo said, stepping between Doc and Jacques.

Jacques and Doc stepped around him to greet Evgenie and Helen.

Gabe put a hand on Jacques shoulder. "What you being so impolite for? We got things to get clear hear, about who's running things and how and you need to listen up!"

"Stuff it, Gabe," Helen said, standing with her feet spread and her arms folded.

Dominic Oporto trotted up behind Gabe. "Something wrong?"

Jacques noted that they'd found themselves in two groups. Gabe, Leo, and Dominic with Edith and Maria cowering nervously behind them, facing Jacques, Doc, Evgenie, Helen and Collette. Arroya and Soob were nowhere to be seen.

"Aw, nuts," Gabe said. "Look, we had a kind of election and I got myself elected mayor. It's no big deal and if you want to have another election, I guess that's all right."

"Are you sure?" Dominic asked.

"God will take care of it," Gabe said.

"Okay, okay," Leo said. "Look, we had a discussion about where we're going, what we're going to do, and why. Maybe we should have waited for you two, but there it is."

"More of a bunch of assertions than a discussion," Doc said. "With some of us a little too busy to participate fully."

"If you let me tell you what we've found out," Jacques said, "I think it will give us a better idea of what to do next. Now please give me a little room; I'm going to draw in the sand."

With some grumbling from Leo, they backed off and Jacques drew a square with his staff.

"All the land we can see is in the form of what looks to be a pretty geometric square. Now the gravity field is radially symmetric so the atmosphere and ocean surface are spherical. So the corners of the square stick up out of the atmosphere and the oceans bulge out of the center a bit." He drew a circle inside the square. "The breathable air would be limited to a radius of something like this a few hundred kilometers from the center, where we are."

He drew a tiny circle in the center. "We are on a roughly circular island, maybe a hundred twenty or thirty kilometers across, with a crater lake in the middle."

He drew another pair of nested circles, leaving what looked like an archery target inside the square. "It's surrounded by forest and grassland; more forest to the east, more grassland to the west, down to the ocean shore."

"The ocean is maybe three hundred and fifty kilometers wide. There's forest on the other side, thinning out more and more as it moves out and the air gets thinner. There's snow or frost just inside the breathable atmosphere ring, then it gets pretty bare beyond that. The land looks pretty flat to the naked eye, but I got some binoculars powered up, and it's actually pretty rough–almost terraced as you go further out."

"I don't see how this can be an accident," Collette added. "I think it's a designed place."

"The whole universe is a designed place," Gabe said.

There was a moment of tense silence. "Well, this looks like it's a little more designed than usual, Gabe," Doc said, to muffled laughter, "by someone or something with a bit of an artistic sense, or maybe a sense of humor. Jacques, you don't suppose the whole world could be a cube, do you?"

"That's ridiculous," Dominic said. "This is all just a trick of perspective. Out in space, it probably doesn't even look square. We're just in a huge crater, like Hellas on Mars, and the rim just happens to look like this from the center."

"Well, maybe," Helen said. "In any event, we're on a volcanic pimple at the bottom of a bowl, gravitationally speaking, summer is starting, and it's already forty in the shade. We're better able to stand heat than our ancestors, but still we should be thinking of moving elsewhere."

"You seem to be comfortable enough with heat," Gabe said, getting chuckles from Dominic and Leo, and a bit of titter from Edith. "Seriously, we've put a lot of work into this here new town, and *if* we credit what Jacques' saying, in a few days we'll be past periwhatever and it will start getting cooler."

Helen shook her head. "No, it won't. Thermal lag, Gabe. Especially with an atmosphere this thick and massive. This is the start of local summer. Maria, I think you have something to say?"

Gabe frowned at Helen, but Maria, hesitantly, stepped forward. When she was rescued she was chatty and exuberant. What, Jacques wondered had happened in three days?

"There are only two kinds of tall trees in the forest," Maria said. "Both are well adapted to fire. It's been dry for the last ten days or so. The brush plants, edenhemp, tanglegrass, ablecane, and others have gone to seed and are drying out. The dinoroos have vanished and we haven't seen a spinyball for days. I... I think things are getting ready for a fire. It's probably part of the natural life cycle here."

"Well, we can wait it out," Gabe said. "We got all we need right here with the lake."

"Not exactly," Doc said. "I can't do a proper analysis, but we're probably getting a lot of what we need from the plants we've been eating. Ascorbic acid definitely–nobody's getting scurvy and we've been here about long enough."

"Aw, that's just a pointy headed theory of yours," Gabe said. "You don't have an AI to ask."

"If the fire starts while we go through the forest," Dominic said urgently, "then we're in for a real disaster! I think we're safer here. Like Gabe says." He smiled at Gabe

Gabe smiled back.

"This is an active volcano," Helen said. "And we're near at the point of maximum tidal stress."

Jacques looked at the north side of the caldera. What he remembered as wisps of steam had become a fairly constant cloud.

Gabe groaned. "Aw, bullfeathers! We could wait a million years for an eruption!"

"Or an hour," Doc said.

"Has anyone seen Soob?" Jacques asked.

"He's still hunting," Gabe said. "I had to come back and get things organized."

And it just so happened he wasn't there to oppose you, Jacques thought. "Where were you?" he asked.

Gabe waved a hand toward the north. "Down by where my CSU crashed. Hunting's better."

"It's getting dark," Leo said. "Let's say a prayer for him tonight and discuss what we're going to do. We can send a search party at first light tomorrow." He stared right at Jacques.

Do I challenge him? Jacques asked himself. Not over something that he's right about. "Okay, let's talk."

"Tell him, Gabe," Leo said.

"Yes, tell him," Dominic said.

"We need to think about what kind of life we're going to make here," Gabe said. "Now, I'm no New Reformationist myself; I'd been a real Christian for seventy years before I joined this expedition. But if you take away all that nonsense about the face on Mars, they have some ideas about how to organize a colonial agricultural society that really work."

"Like keeping women in their place?" Collette asked.

"There's a natural division of labor; it's in our genetic makeup. Child rearing, making clothes, domestic stuff and all that. Most women want it that way."

"Well, I don't," Collette said.

"Okay, well, so maybe we make a few exceptions to start with. Now there needs to be some firm secular authority. We can't be forever debating on what to do. And there needs to be some spiritual authority, too, someone to remind us that we're human beings made in God's image."

Doc cleared his throat, and said very softly and mildly, "I'm not going to practice or pay lip service to your religion."

Gabe waved his hands, "And I wouldn't want to make you do so. But now just think downstream a little. We get ourselves all sorts of kids and kids can be unruly if they aren't afraid they're going to get caught. Even adults; God knows what we'd do if we didn't know someone was watching us, and judging us!"

"The golden rule gives me a sufficient standard," Helen said. "The laws of the physical universe show us the consequences of our actions to others, and to ourselves."

"But we don't all have Ph.Ds in physics. What's going to keep everyone else in line? We need, I say we need, some kind of religion, something to scare people to do the right thing that can't think it through themselves all the time. I mean what's it going to be like when we have a thousand, ten thousand people here? What's going to keep them all in line?"

Jacques' patience was wearing thin. "We are not going to stay here and found a colony. We are going to recover our technology, build a starship, and go home."

"But how are we going to do that?" Dominic asked. "It's not possible. We've got one wrist comp and solar array that's just barely working. There are only a dozen of us. We have to spend most of our time just finding enough to eat and keep from being dragonoid meat. Be realistic. Maybe in a few years, some of us will have some spare time to work on the problem. Meantime, we need to accept reality. I think Gabe can give us some real common sense leadership, and we're going to need that to get through this."

This was the same man who, just days ago, had so emotionally stated his commitment to finishing their mission! Jacques wanted to tell him about the shuttle, but realized that would reveal his knowledge to the saboteur.

"I think someone who doesn't have a religious agenda would be more appropriate," Doc Yu said. "Helen, for instance."

Gabe shot him a look of pure contempt. "An atheist nudist? You expect *me* to follow *that*!"

Helen laughed. "No, I don't suppose you would. Perhaps we can compromise. Gabe has the energy and desire to organize things. So he can be our CEO. But we can be the board and vote on policy matters, and I would think Jacques should be our chairman. Can we make that work?"

"It seems a lot more complicated than we have time for," Dominic said.

"Do you want to split the community already?" Doc said.

"Do you?" Dominic retorted.

Leo touched Gabe's arm. Gabe nodded and opened his mouth but before he could say anything, a new voice echoed off the rocks.

"Hello, everyone, someone give me a hand!" It was Soob, from somewhere in the dark.

Jacques ran into the shadows toward the voice and found the missing hunter dragging the better part of a kangasaur carcass on a travois of blackwood branches.

"It seemed confused, running toward the fire," he shrugged. "It was going to die anyway. So I speared it and dragged it across the river before the flames got to me."

"What fire?" Maria asked.

"Don't you see it? It's huge. Look at the sky glow over the caldera rim. The whole north slope is going up!"

# CHAPTER 10
# OUT OF THE FRYING PAN

Jacques stared at the flames and tried to calculate how long it would take them to spread around the rim of the caldera. If his guess about the ecology was right, the large trees themselves had evolved to tolerate the fire; it would be mainly the smaller brush that was burning. Flames would be less likely to jump gullies and creeks than similar fire back on Earth.

"Oh, my God!" Gabe said, and stared at the glowing sky. "Well, that settles it. We have to stay here where we're safe. It's a sign, I believe."

"I don't recommend that," Doc said. "We'd be trapped without an adequate food supply."

"At the risk of repeating myself, we should get out of this caldera," Helen said.

"That, apparently, is what the rest of the animal life in these parts has done," Soob added.

"We aren't animals and if Gabe says we stay, we stay," Leo said. "He's our leader."

There was a moment of silence, broken by Edith Lu. "I don't think that has been decided," she said, very hesitantly. Leo shot a look at her.

It was then that the slow drift of air brought the first smell of fire. Jacques looked around. "Deliverance Creek hasn't gone dry yet. We should be able to follow that down to the coast; there are a number of kangasaur trails paralleling it."

"You shut up!" Leo said, and raised his staff. The smaller man's eyes bored into him.

"What?" Jacques said, dumbfounded at the threat of violence.

"Now just hold on a minute here, both of you!" Gabe said. "We can't go anywhere tonight. Let me sleep on it. Maybe it'll look different in the morning, after you two cool off."

"Jacques doesn't need to cool off," Doc said quietly. "He didn't do anything. Leo staged that to give you an opportunity to look like a leader."

Everyone looked at Leo, who just stood there with his hands tight around his staff. Jacques spoke into the awkward pause. "We have plenty of light to see the trail," he said, waving a hand at the sky glow. Let's gather things up and get going. We can spend the night at Rim Cave."

"Too risky," Gabe said. "Dragons up there."

Dominic Oporto shook his head. "I'm with Gabe. I'm not going out there to get fried just on the chance the volcano might burp. We can eat fish until the fire's over."

There was another long silence, with people staring at each other. Leo brought his staff down slowly and Jacques took a deep breath. His own hands, he noted, had clenched into fists with such force that his fingernails had dug into his palms. Low gravity beside the point, weeks of unremitting physical labor had hardened his body. Staff or not, he probably would have little trouble in a physical confrontation with Leo; perhaps what was in the other man's eyes was as much fear as anger.

"You need more than fish," Doc said.

"Perhaps splitting up is not such a bad idea," Helen said. "If there is risk in both directions, our overall odds of survival are better if we try both. Assuming even odds, that would give an overall probability of success of 75%. The successful group can rescue the other, if need be."

"The question is who's in charge," Leo said. "I say it's Gabe, and if you walk out on him, you're gone and don't look for any rescue."

"I really believe we're better off staying together here," Oporto said. "I just know it."

Gabe nodded and waved an arm. "Okay. My decision is to stay."

Jacques looked around. Collette, and Soob had already gone back into the cave to gather things. Helen turned and walked in that direction as well. That left him, Gabe, Leo, Dominic, Maria, Arroya, Doc and Edith. Maria looked down, not meeting his eyes. Edith looked to be on the verge of tears, but stayed where she was. Gabe and Leo, Jacques thought, had chosen their own fate, but he felt responsible in some way for the rest.

"Arroya?"

She was looking at Collette, almost in fear. She shook her head sharply.

Evgenie attempted to dissuade her, but she wouldn't move. "I need to stay with her," he said.

"Edith?" he asked.

She glanced at Collette, then looked down at the ground. She'd had her heart set on him, and he, in her mind, had deserted her for Collette. Jacques felt awful, but was unable to give Edith what she wanted.

Doc walked over to Jacques, put a hand on his back, and nodded to the cave. Jacques followed him. The sooner gone the better, he decided.

When they emerged, set for their journey, the remaining group made no quarrel with the division of the few common resources, and pretty much ignored them. Except Gabe, who walked with them to the trail head.

"Are you sure you won't reconsider?" he said, motioning to the glowing red sky. "Looks pretty hot out there."

Jacques hesitated. Was Gabe a saboteur and a murderer? Somehow Jacques didn't think so; the man seemed too sure of himself and his beliefs to stoop to such tactics. Should he warn Gabe that among those remaining was probably the author of their entire situation?

Yet Gabe might still be that person himself. Or Leo, hiding behind Gabe. Or someone hiding from the group. Or anyone, Jacques thought. With a surreptitious power source, even the people they'd pulled from the CSUs could have gone out and in again, he thought. His next thought was that he was getting paranoid.

He shook his head and without another word turned and headed for the ridge. He did not look back, even when he heard Edith sob.

∞◇∞

The scene when they reached the rim, about local midnight, was surrealistic; the inferno from the North side of the caldera had extended fangs of fire into the area between the rim and the sea–a vast glowing upper jaw. Underlit red and gold clouds laced with black and gray roiled into the sky above. The air smelled of soot and a dull crackling roar, still distant, banished silence.

"We shouldn't stop to sleep," Helen said, clearly appalled at the scene to the north. "The coast could be a day or two away, even at a downhill lope."

"I think Jacques has something else in mind," Collette said.

Jacques shook his head. "Not unless we're very lucky. There's a river valley to our south that we can follow down. It hasn't gone dry; I think it's fed by the lake in the caldera through an underground passage. There are pools along the way. If the fire catches us, we duck. The slope flattens out toward the coast; I'm hoping for better foraging there."

"And what if we get lucky?" Soob asked.

Should he tell them? What if one of them decided to go back to Gabe?

You can't avoid all risk, he decided. "We get a megabat to give us a lift." Jacques recounted the flight he and Collette had taken. "We're a lot quicker than they are; they're basically carrion eaters, not hunters. I'm hoping the misfortune of some kangasaurs along the way will prove our fortune. It takes some nerve but once you get on, you can steer them by pulling on their ears."

"You're serious?" Doc said.

"He certainly is!" Collette said.

"Okay, okay." He shook his head. "We should take at least a couple of hours rest here; we'll get the time back by being more alert and making better decisions on the trail below."

There was general assent to that and people headed for the cave. Inside, Jacques went to where he had hidden his electronics. Did he want to lug Ascendant's CSU control module along with everything else? He decided not to; he knew what was on it. But he did pull its memory chip; the shuttle computer might be able to get more out of it than he could. With that done, he turned in, about an hour later than everyone else.

∞◇∞

Morning was like waking up in an oven. The smell of smoke was everywhere now, and the sky was a red blanket, lit from beneath by the fires in the north and only somewhat lighter in the direction of the sun. Jacques assembled the small group for the dash to the sea. It was 48 C at 3600 plus millibars. Fortunately, there was plenty of water, even if it was warm. Everyone was quiet and apprehensive; the next two days would likely test them physically and mentally as nothing in their lives had ever done.

But before they left, Collette wanted to have a word with everyone.

"As some of you know, or have figured out, Ascendant Chryse was murdered."

"What?!" Helen exclaimed.

Doc simply nodded, and Jacques had already told Soob.

"She was camping in her CSU. Someone came by at night and cut the power from outside, locking her in and suffocating her. Whoever it was left fingerprints on the control module and the sides of the CSU." Collette held up a small thick rectangular card, about half the size of the palm of her hand. "My micro crime lab. It does fingerprints, voice recognition, DNA matching, and a number of other things."

Jacques stared at her. He knew she was a policewoman, but had just assumed that circumstances had left that far behind. But if he looked back, there were clues. The long time she'd spent on the hunt before they'd taken the ride on the megabat. The careful attention she'd paid to everything. He gulped, suddenly realizing his own prints were all over Ascendant's camp site.

"It's not an AI, Jacques. I wouldn't have held back on something useful. Anyway, the same person may have been responsible for the sabotage of our mission and our present predicament. I'm ninety percent certain it was nobody in this group."

"We were all under water!" Soob said.

"One can swim up and down from a submerged CSU, as long as it has enough power. And our perpetrator would have been able to plan in advance. What I'd like everyone to do now is to come up and touch the mini-lab. We all need to trust each other, and be sure. Then I'll explain everything. Jacques?"

"But my prints are all over her CSU!"

"Two days after she expired, and during the day."

"That can tell the difference?" Soob asked, in wonderment.

"It can date fresh prints within about twelve percent. I already have Jacques' prints." She smiled at him. "Soob?"

He shrugged, walked up and touched the device where Collette indicated. Helen and Doc followed. There were no matches.

"Now I hope we get to hear what this is all about," Helen said.

Collette nodded to Jacques.

"Okay. There's an intact starship shuttle on this planet," he said, and pointed west. "That way. We think we can take control of it, if we can reach it physically."

"Then we'd best get going," Doc said.

∞◇∞

They jogged, rested at a walking pace, and jogged again. The high oxygen content and the downhill slope helped; however, their lack of calories made them tire easily. As the day wore on they spent less time jogging and more time walking. The kangasaur path that roughly paralleled Deliverance Creek grew wider as they descended.

"It's almost like a river itself," Soob remarked during a water break at the creeks edge. "Other paths join it."

"A migration, path, maybe," Jacques noted. He wanted to sleep. More than anything else, he wanted to sleep. The sun had probably set, but with the fire glow lighting the sky, it was hard to tell.

"Dry down here," Helen said, snapping a desiccated flute plant stem. "Hot." She ducked out of her bag, pulled her boots off, and picked her way into the creek. It still ran vigorously, but it was easy for Jacques to see where its normal boundaries were.

"I'd join you, but I'm too tired," Collette said.

"Listen," Doc said. "That crackling noise. The fire must be getting near."

Three hundred meters upstream, a stand of flute plant burst into flames, without any spark that anyone could see. Quickly, its neighbors caught fire.

"Let's get in the creek." Soob said.

But Helen, who was already in, did the opposite. "It will be filled with burning logs in minutes. I think we have to run for it."

For the moment, fear banished fatigue, and soon they were jogging down the trail again.

But in a few minutes, the adrenaline rush ran out. Fantasies of heroic leadership dying, it was Jacques, himself, who hit the wall first. Perhaps because he was a bit larger, or because he'd been subsisting on a native diet longer, or perhaps because he'd had less sleep. Or all of that.

"I can't go on," he said as he collapsed. "Muscles won't move."

Doc came back for him and pressed a small patch on his arm. "Only a few of these," he said. "I've saved them for emergencies. It should give you another couple hours, then you're out."

Jacques felt a sort of coolness flow through his body. He shivered, then found he could stand. Doc looked at him and nodded. Two hours would not be enough, and they both knew it.

An hour and half later, Jacques started to slow down again. The world reeled around him. "Collette," he tried to call out, but it was only a whisper.

Soob saw him stumble and came back to aid him and called for Doc to help.

"Eureka!" Helen yelled from somewhere in front of them. "It's a lake!"

"Come on, guy," Doc said. "Just another hundred yards or so."

Later, Jacques would swear that Doc said that at least five times before he fell into the water.

Walls of flame rose around him as he was towed to a hillock of pahoehoe lava in the lake. It was free of vegetation–probably underwater most of the year. The smooth rock felt cool on his back as he lost consciousness.

# CHAPTER 11
# FLIGHT

Jacques woke to devastation. In place of trees, skeletons of white ash stood like ghostly Ents beyond the shores of their refuge. The forest floor was as white as if covered by snow. The sky above was gray now, though red tinged toward the west horizon. The air smelled, and even tasted, burnt.

"Good morning," Soob said, from somewhere behind him. "Doc caught something!"

It looked vaguely like a catfish with three sets of lobed fins and a horizontal tail.

"I hope you like sushi," Collette added.

There was, Jacques realized, nothing combustible left within many kilometers to cook with.

The meal was woefully inadequate, but too much better than nothing to complain. They ate it silently, packed up, forded the lake and headed west. With no point in hurrying any longer, they tried to move as efficiently as possible.

"Another day," Helen said, then asked, calmly, "Are we going to last another day?"

The ground crunched beneath their boots and staffs as clouds of ash flew up to coat their bodies. They passed a scorched Kangasaur.

Someone I knew? Jacques asked himself, but he didn't have the energy to examine it closer.

"Think about lasting another five minutes. Then do that again." Doc whispered.

Jacques' vision focused on the ground ahead of him. Not five minutes, but one more step.

No! He shook himself. He could not give up; he was supposed to be their leader. He had to think ahead, see ahead. Angry with himself, he straightened up and looked around and up. Then he saw the shadow coming down at them.

"Megabat," he croaked. "Overhead."

"Another one, to our right!" Soob pointed. "Two. Three."

All over the sky, huge black crescents emerged from the haze, gliding downward.

"Appears they've just been invited to a barbie," Soob said.

There was nowhere to hide or take cover, absolutely nowhere. The megabat Jacques saw got lower and lower, headed directly for them. Too exhausted to run, they huddled together, with Collette, who seemed strongest, in front. The great beak on its thick neck opened wide and Collette waved her staff at it—a disparity in force so incredible that it would have been humorous but for the desperation of their situation.

Then, with a downbeat of its wings that sent ash flying up all around them, the monster sailed over them for the dead Kangasaur upstream.

"It's about ten times our combined mass and no resistance," Helen observed.

Jacques found his voice. "Collette, if we can get on that thing..."

Doc and Helen looked at him as if he were crazy, but Soob, the hunter, smiled.

"It's busy with the kangasaur," he said. "It would hardly notice us if we jump up on it."

"I can barely lift my arms, let alone jump," Helen said.

Doc reached into his pack for a couple of boost patches. "I don't think any of us are in shape to do much jumping. But if two of us take these, we'll be able to help the others on."

"We can rope ourselves together," Helen suggested. "Collette, you've done this before. Jacques shouldn't have another dose, Doc has to monitor us, and Soob, you're stronger than I am. It should be Soob and Collette, I think."

Everyone murmured an assent. Collette was already into her kit. "We should put our suits on, too. Hard to believe now, but it can get cool up there."

Moving as quickly as they could, they washed off in the river. Lack of towels was no problem—in the desiccated air, they were dry by the time they climbed back up to the trail. Once in the suits, except for the long beards on the men, they looked civilized again. Along with that, having their fill of water to drink and the anticipation of the upcoming adventure raised spirits. Doc administered the drug to Collette and Soob. Then they all approached the feeding monster from behind. It had been diligent; the Kangasaur was half gone.

The megabat shivered slightly as Collette clambered up its stubby tail and onto its hindquarters, but didn't pause from its grisly meal. One by one the rest of the party followed, stepping into Soob's hands to be boosted—essentially to be thrown, onto the megabat back. Then there was nothing to do but wait.

Helen and Soob were already asleep in the soft fur between the megabat's shoulders, safely secured between Doc and Helen, when it decided it was satiated and took flight. Jacques grabbed the fur and stuck his head up. Collette was on the beast's neck, ready to try to guide it toward the ocean.

But that proved unnecessary. Riding on a powerful updraft from the fire, the megabat gained a tremendous altitude, then headed for the far shoreline on its own. Amazingly, except for the smoke and haze over the island, the entire sky seemed devoid of clouds. The land below was a perfect square, the ocean a huge circle inside of it, and the island a target in its center. Megabats—Jacques estimated perhaps as many as a hundred—circled over it, not unlike buzzards over a corpse in a desert though the scale was a hundred times larger. On the shoreline, still green and moist, he saw kangasaurs in the surf, fishing like bears with great swipes of their forearms. Then the shore passed beneath him, and soon they were over a vast ocean.

Collette released her hold on the monster's ear, worked her way back, settled beside him and roped herself to him. They kissed briefly and she fell asleep. Too far out to think about swimming back, they were going wherever this megabat was going.

∞◇∞

Two hours out over the ocean, when Collette and Soob revived enough to listen, Helen held forth. She had rigged a circle of lines on the megabat's back by braiding patches of megabat hair into short ropes that could be knotted to their lines. With this, everyone felt more secure, though the megabat had hardly tilted at all during the flight.

"So I think Doc's cube world idea is correct," she concluded.

"On this side, anyway," Soob said, "the biosphere is a fluid bulge on a square face."

"Indeed," Helen responded. "The ocean and the atmosphere respond to gravity, and intersect the cube in circles. See how the snow line curves up toward the mountain peaks? If there were only four mountains, the thing would be unbalanced, I think. It works better as a sphere with eight huge mountains the shape of triangular pyramids, arranged symmetrically."

"Why don't the mountains collapse?" Soob asked. "My memory is a little hazy, but I thought planets this size would inevitably assume a more or less spherical form."

Helen shook her head. "They should. I can only guess that the mountains are made of something very strong and light weight. *Made* is the operative word. I think this is a manufactured world."

"But why would anyone do this" Collette asked.

"The mountains, and the ridges connecting their peaks, extend beyond the atmosphere," Soob observed.

Helen nodded. "All but the last traces. Each face of the cube would be isolated from the other faces, for things not able to travel through vacuum. It could harbor six separate biomes, but each with the same insolation and resources."

"A zoo?" Jacques speculated. "With life forms from different worlds?"

"You wouldn't need a perfect cube for that," Soob said. "I suspect some aesthetic motivation as well—form and function. It's architecture on a scale we've only began to think about. I'd like to meet whoever came up with this."

Everyone fell silent at that point, gazing at the incredible sight below them. Jacques felt an unjustified, giddy relief. Saboteurs, murderers, and fire lay behind them. In the alien forests and cliffs ahead of them, somewhere, was a link to the civilization they had lost. If they could find it. If they could feed themselves. If they could avoid being eaten.

# CHAPTER 12
# AT THE EDGE OF FOREVER

Hours passed and the western shore came into view, then passed beneath them. The land, so flat from a distance, was anything but as they neared it—filled with terraces, gulches, waterfalls and ridges. Their approach was disorienting. Their eyes told them the megabat was diving down into a roughly flat landscape, while all their other senses told them it was flying level.

"Keep thinking 'mountainside'," Doc said. "Or you could get sick. Look at the angle the trees make with the land."

That helped quiet Jacques' stomach, at least. But the fact that they could see individual trees also rang an alarm bell. Whether descending, or flying into a mountainside, they were rapidly approaching the end of their flight.

"We need to get ready to get off!" he shouted. "We'll need to run for the trees, or someone will be its next snack."

Though famished, everyone was well rested. They quickly untied the lines, stowed them, and helped each other strap on their kits. The megabat settled down in the tree-crowned top of a huge pillar that had become slightly detached from a terrace cliff. As it settled down in a clearing, a number of much smaller versions of itself—each still twice as large as a person—came hopping out of the surrounding wood to greet it. That proved more than enough distraction for the humans to jump off and run for shelter.

"Okay, gang," Collette said, on catching her breath. "We've eaten one tiny meal in two days and we're trapped on a sky island plateau filled with huge predators? Why do I feel like I just got out of school?"

"Stress relief," Doc said. "We still have big problems, but they aren't immediate problems."

Everyone laughed. Something scurried away–a hirachnoid.

"Dinner, anyone?" Soob asked.

"We need a place to sleep and I don't see anything resembling a cave," Collette observed.

"The trees are different here," Jacques noted, thinking aloud. "They have more branches, and a wider crown. There might be a place to build a platform. Over there." He pointed to a tree with wrinkled gray bark and two lower branches that came out at almost the same level, about three meters up. "Okay. Soob, Collette, and Doc, why don't you forage. Helen and I will try to make a platform for us."

As the hunter-gatherers left on their mission, Jacques and Helen constructed the nest, using the nearly indestructible line from Helen's emergency kit to make a web between the branches. They filled that web with whatever branches they could find lying around and secured those with a local vine, that, while not green twine, served almost as well. Helen called it pseudotwine. Jacques left the construction to Helen while he gathered material.

"Come on up," Helen said, throwing down a pseudotwine vine tied to an overhead branch. He pulled himself up easily hand over hand in the low gravity and lowered himself onto the platform; it was springy, but didn't feel like it was going anywhere.

Still, he felt better sitting down. Helen had resumed her customary state and stowed her shipsuit in her kit, which was hanging from an overhead branch. She waved at it, saying, "Save the suits for when we need them."

Despite having gone unclothed, or nearly so, for over a month, having been clothed for a few hours had put Jacques back into another cultural mode, and he hesitated. With a sly smile, Helen reached over and, starting at his collar, began to peel his suit off like a banana skin.

When she got it off him, she began to cuddle. "Time for dessert," she said.

He laughed and gently pushed her away. "Too tired Helen. I'm just too worn out."

∞◇∞

They spent the next few days resting, hiding from megabats, and foraging. The clear day of their arrival proved a fortunate rarity; more typical were misty mornings and gentle midday showers. It was more temperate here, with daytime temperatures in the high 20s; air pressure was down to around 3000 millibars and more variable than at New Landing. The view from the tree was to die for. But a week after their arrival, they were rested and provisioned; it was time to move on.

They packed up camp at noon the next day, with the megabats safely in their daily slumber, and explored the western edge of their sky island, looking for a way across the gap.

"It's like Meteora, in Greece," Helen said. "Except ten times bigger. People built monasteries on top of natural pillars like this; they looked impossible to get to. The megabats keep their chicks here for the same reason, I think. But there is usually a back way, a thin bridge or connection with the rest of the plateau; not an easy way, but much more negotiable than the sheer fronts and sides. We just have to find it."

Jacques spotted it on the second day of looking, toward the south side of the pillar. About three hundred meters below the plateau, flutes from the pillar and plateau extended to meet each other. Almost. There was a gap of perhaps ten meters, with a treacherous narrow ridge leading to it on either side.

"Everyone. Over here," he called.

"An easy jump in this gravity," Soob said as he arrived, surveying the gap. "But staying where you land, maybe not so easy."

"There's a tree about four meters up," Colette said. "I was a long jumper in college. I think I can make it with a rope around my waist."

"Remember the air is three times thicker here," Doc said. "You'll lose speed quickly."

"What about a bridge?" Helen asked. "There are logs long enough, and we have line."

"Hmmm," Jacques said.

It was, possibly, the first suspension bridge on the planet; certainly the first human-built one. They used two twelve-meter logs; the first was erected vertically on the sky island side, set in a hole and held in place by rocks piled around it. A line, anchored to a tree, went over its top and was tied to the far end of the other log. This they pushed out over the gap, playing the line out as it went until it hung swaying over the far end. They anchored the near end with a pile of rocks, then raised and lowered the far end onto the far side of the chasm until it had pounded a secure groove for itself in the loose soil there. The party crossed one at a time, with lines around their waists in case they slipped.

To get up the gravel on the other side, they made a human road to the nearest tree. Doc lay down on the slope with his feet securely on the log. Jacques crawled up over him and, with Doc's help, placed his feet on Doc's shoulders and lay down, extending the human road another meter and a half. Helen followed, and then Collette with a line which she tied to the tree toehold on the plateau. Using the bridge and ropes, they got their gear across the gap and up to the level part of the plateau. It took them most of the day. They made camp on a secure flat near the edge of the cliff. It was somewhat risky, but they were beyond tired and the view of sea cliffs below, the sea, and the top of the mist-shrouded island they'd fled was to die for.

"It's like we're on the edge of forever," Doc said.

The next morning, Jacques put up a cairn and on the more or less flat face of a rock, scratched their names and:

Day 54: Camp Edge of Forever.

∞◊∞

The plateau proved to be one of the terraces Jacques had seen from the far shore; three kilometers in, they were faced with a kilometer-tall rock face.

"In this gravity, a piece of cake," Collette said, looking at the rough, crevice-filled rock face. She showed them how to jam flute plant stems in cracks as big, ersatz pitons, and they scaled the thing in a couple of hours.

They had enough provisions for three days' climb, which took them up over a half dozen "terraces." Jacques welcomed the break from breaking trail through the forest and the view at the top of each cliff. If they found an exceptionally tall tree at the top of a cliff, they would climb it and look back. The ocean would cover the eastern horizon, perhaps slightly bowed upward as it conformed to gravity and not the flat topography. In the far east, they could see a dark smudge, so small now that they could cover it with a hand. Smoke still rose from it like a strange plant with wispy gray leaves reaching impossibly high into the sky.

Jacques assembled his electronic gear and waited for the sun to peek through the clouds and provide the power he needed. When they got another bearing to the shuttle, it was west and south of where they were. The signal had increased in strength, but not as much as he would have expected from the ocean crossing.

Each day Jacques took readings; a hundred meters left, a hundred right. They were headed toward the shuttle, but the signal was not getting much stronger.

Meanwhile, the flora and fauna changed. The broad fleshy-leafed bitterwood tree was giving way to a very tall tree with a rough yellowish bark that covered its trunk and limbs like scales. Its foliage seemed to come from a simple modification of the bark; the scales appeared to curl into finger-sized hollow tubes.

Helen picked a leaf up from the forest floor. "The underside's translucent," she noted. "I'll bet it's a good insulator."

"Winter adaptation?" Soob asked.

Jacques nodded and stretched his hand out and covered their sun with his thumb. In the week since arriving at Camp Edge of Forever the star had gotten noticeably smaller. "Our sun is shrinking."

"Apastron?" Collette asked.

Jacques frowned. He didn't think they'd reached the furthest point of their planet's orbit yet, but it was hard to tell how long it would be. "Not yet, but we're well past periastron now. It's not just the gain in altitude that's making us chilly."

Soob nodded. "We'll need to find a good campsite, one where we can settle long enough to make some winter clothes."

Helen laughed, then looked very thoughtful. At length she said, "We all still hope to find the shuttle, recover all our technology, and continue our mission. But it might not work out that way."

"You're suggesting we locate a permanent settlement site here?" Doc asked.

Helen nodded. "At least a base camp. We'll need to stop at a place that's survivable with what we have."

"We still have a mission," Colette said.

The quiet that ensued spoke of the elephant in the room. The urgency of the quest to find the shuttle had, necessarily, abated and he imagined that everyone was thinking like he was, though not saying it. Those that had stayed behind had either survived or not–either way, they would hardly need rescuing now. Building a new starship was a very long term

project–and they had been striving for all they were worth for almost a month now. It was time to scale back to a sustainable pace.

"Maybe the next likely place after a week's climb?" he said. "That will give us a week to get ready for apastron, and the season will likely lag."

There were assents all the way around.

# CHAPTER 13
# EAGLE'S NEST

They had settled into a routine, gaining about twelve kilometers a day horizontally and four vertically. At first light they were up, ate a hearty breakfast, and packed away the remaining food. Then they did four terraces, with a water break after scaling the second cliff of the day. During the break, they would recharge their electronics. The hard part of the day was the next two traverse and climbs. They would take a long rest after the fourth climb, then build camp and forage. After the sun went down, they'd have a light dinner by the fire and go to sleep, taking watch shifts.

Jacques had just gone over the top of the fourth terrace on the day's climb. The trees he saw seemed larger and further apart than below; the effect was almost park-like. He gazed up at one giant that came up from near the terrace edge; it seemed almost twenty meters across and actually vanished into a wisp of cloud above him.

Trying to find its top, he wasn't looking where he was going and about thirty meters in from the terrace edge, he saw a small pit too late and felt the sandy ground give way under him. He tried to scramble back, but the ground gave way faster. "Falling! Belay!" he yelled as he slipped beneath the surface. His belay line pulled taut, and he soon found himself dangling about five meters below the surface in a huge cave. Below him was a pile of sharp rocks, many as big as small houses. Lava tube, he thought, when he stopped shuddering. The ceiling must have caved in here a long time ago—forest debris had almost filled in the hole. As his eyes adapted to the light, he could see that the volume around him was immense; the cave must have been a hundred meters across in places. He could hear a small stream running through it.

Water supply, drainage, shelter, defendable... he ticked through various plusses."Soob," he yelled. "Soob. I think I've found it!"

When the group all reached the hole, they descended on ropes and explored the cave. It led toward the face of the terrace, and as it did, the floor became smoother, like the dried bottom of a creek. The creek itself ended in a pool.

Helen shook her head. "I can feel wind. The terrace face must be within a few meters of us."

Colette nodded. "The pile of dirt across the pool—it's not lava. It looks like it came this way, inward from the face, not down the tube." She waded through the pool and climbed up it, toward the cave roof. Suddenly she thrust her arm into the wall, and brought it back holding a large white flower. "We have a window!"

They built "Eagles Nest" over the next week, enlarging the silted up window and leveling the floor behind it until they had an opening ten meters long and a meter high toward the east. For in the morning, the rising sun, if visible, would fill the cave with light back to the skylight fall. They built a rough stone wall at the edge of that; for defense and to keep from falling off; the terrace edge was slightly undercut, and the drop to the next level must have a kilometer.

On the second day, Soob and Jacques were hunting. The hirachnoids were larger at this altitude, with thicker legs, though Helen thought they weren't as sweet as on the island. Jacques had a couple sets of legs in his bag when he noticed the smell.

"Jacques, something's dead, " Soob said.

"I'd say so."

"Hirachnoids are scavengers," Soob added.

"I was afraid you would mention that."

Following their noses, they found a megabat carcass, maybe three days old. Hirachnoids were going in and out of its cloacal opening, now somewhat enlarged, covered with little bits of what had been inside.

"I'm going to be sick," Jacques said, and turned to retch. When he was over it, he turned back to see Soob busy slicing away the webbing of the carcass's right wing.

"Fur coats," Soob said. "I don't think it's been above ten Celsius since we got here."

Disgust aside, Jacques realized that fate had handed them a treasure trove. He quickly went to help. Soon, they had all the wing web pelt they could carry. Just as well, he thought, with a glance at one of the large, glistening hirachnoids.

They dug an outlet for the pond and rigged a flood gate for it. All that nice smooth silt had come from somewhere, and they didn't want to be washed away by the next rainy season. They found a "bottomless" crack near the cave mouth across the pond from their camp. With a short stone wall for privacy, it would now have its share of bottoms.

It snowed on the morning of the third day, in huge flakes as big as their hands. Almost ten centimeters of soft white snow built up in about no time, but it quickly melted. The storm did show them that the cave was too drafty, so they wove a barrier out of yellowbark branches that they could use to cover the entrance at night.

The long days were full of unending labor; every fallen log from several kilometers around found its way down the skylight. Everything edible they could find went into the hole, too. Jacques figured they had about fifteen days of supplies when winter hit in earnest.

It snowed heavily on the fourth day of occupying Eagles Nest, gusts of wind bringing flakes through the cave. Despite their barrier, the freezing wind found its way to them and they huddled close in their blankets. They fed the fire frugally and waited, then finally arranged a fire watch, using a crude water clock as a timer–it let a stone fall when the cup became too light–and slept.

Jacques had the first shift and spent much of it in wonder at how he'd gone from a reasonably prosperous childhood on Cislunar L5 Grissom to his present circumstances. He wondered about his mother and father; where were they now? They'd certainly have given him up for dead, and had likely passed on one way or another themselves.

Did they keep their religion to the end? he wondered. Did they ever regret the beatings? How could one profess love one minute, then scream and hit the next? He had never had children; what happened to him ran in families and he had vowed it would end with him. He was going to have to have an honest talk with Collette.

The rock dropped; surprising him. He put another piece of wood on the fire and blew the embers until it caught, then went to wake Soob for the next shift. He snuggled under his blankets and thought about humankind expanding through the galaxy, wondering how long it would take for them to get this far.

Jacques felt a gentle shaking, opened his eyes and saw Collette, who planted a quick kiss on his cheek.

"It's morning," she said, nodding to the pale light from the cliff face window. "The wind's stopped."

Jacques yawned and pushed himself up. She reached for his hand and he found himself in her arms, naturally, unbidden. Their embrace lasted as long as it needed to—no urgency to it, but a bond renewed. They had become special to each other. Not intentionally, but it had happened. He felt comfortable, warm and at peace in her arms. The conversation could wait, he thought.

"Let's check the entrance," she said.

Jacques smiled, wondering if it was an excuse to get away from the others.

"There's hardly a breeze," she said. "It might be blocked."

Situation awareness, Jacques thought, getting his head back to reality. They were in a survival situation on an alien world. He nodded. "Yeah. We should check."

The vertical entrance was, indeed, completely blocked, a pillar of compressed snow like a white trumpet, bell down, rising from the gnarly cave floor to its ceiling. Only the cliff face window remained open. They were in for the season, it seemed.

∞◇∞

They settled into a routine of sleeping by the fire, eating, and working on small projects. They found a large piece of obsidian, with an edge of about ten centimeters width, that they could use to shave bitterwood logs. They could write on the shavings with wet charcoal, not very finely, but good enough for some haiku and other short poems.

They peeled apart the megabat web skin pelts, scraped away the small amount of flesh between the skin layers, soaked them in water and ash, rinsed them in the pool, then suspended them over the fire until they steamed, hopefully killing any decay-causing bacteria and preserving them for use. They smelled better, anyway.

Cut and folded, with a hole in the center for someone's head and a strip of skin for a belt, the megabat skins made passable ponchos. They were almost impermeable, and the short fur, turned inside, made them comfortable to wear.

They made plans for the next summer's exploration, learned each other's personal histories, and spun many untestable, unobservable theories about Cube World's origins. Doc carved a passable model of the world, complete with the slight bulges for oceans on each face.

Soob made a chess set, and became their local grand master, though Jacques wondered if he would have succeeded so well if Helen had participated in his tournaments. She claimed to not know how to play, but Jacques thought she watched the board with more than casual interest.

Helen spent her time making a wooden necklace of interlaced rings, carved from a single piece of bitterwood branch. It was a topological marvel they all admired.

Many years ago, Jacques had taught himself how to play a Peruvian flute; a simple tube with a slanted notch and holes for an octave's worth of notes. He'd had that in the back of his mind when he named the "flute plant." It was a project, with some cut and try to get the intervals right, but finally they had four passable flutes, two base and two tenor. Helen, Soob, and Collette learned to play, and they eventually managed a truncated, ersatz performance of the New World Symphony, with Doc playing a batskin drum and singing "going home."

They gossiped about their days in training, and various couplings imagined and real.

"Evgenie told me he had a hard time making up his mind about Ascendant," Helen said.

"I thought he was soft on Arroya," Doc said. "And he was dating you, too?"

Helen laughed. "I was his safety valve! I'm a good listener and was obviously not looking for an exclusive relationship."

"When we split," Jacques said, "she was looking at you—almost fearfully, I thought. Any history there?"

Collette shook her head. "Maybe she doesn't like cops. What about Leo?" she asked. "Was he involved with anyone?"

Helen shrugged. "He didn't seem interested in anyone, that I could see."

"Not even you?" Collette smiled when she said that.

Helen laughed. "The lack of interest was mutual. There's something about him... maybe it's stature compensation."

"A Napoleon complex?" Doc offered. "He seems content to let Eddie take the lead. Anyway, I saw him on a Chesapeake Bay cruise with Maria Lopes. She touched him in a pretty friendly fashion. Eddie was there, too, if I recall."

Jacques looked over at Collette, who looked back and frowned. They'd been thinking in terms of one saboteur and murderer; they hadn't considered more than one.

∞◇∞

Ten days from becoming snowbound, Jacques, trailing a tether, squeezed through the narrow horizontal crack of the window, stuck his head out into a freezing wind and looked up fifty meters at an overhang of ice-covered rock, and down to the snow-covered terrace, a kilometer below. To his right there was the bare hint of a ledge, covered with snow—which probably covered ice—that slanted down and then up in the distance toward a notch in the ledge.

It was, he realized, less dangerous than his Earth-gravity-trained intuition told him. But without an ax, crampons or pitons, it was still a suicidal traverse. He wiggled himself back in and, for a moment, the erstwhile cold damp air of the cave felt warm and inviting.

"I think," he told the assembled group, "we're better off attacking the snow pillar."

Three hours later, using the light of improvised torches, they stared up at the barely visible mountain of snow that had drifted down into, and eventually sealed off, the "skylight" entrance to Eagles Nest. Somewhere in there was the rope they had used to come in and out.

Soob attempted climbing up the snow hill and sank up to his crotch. As he attempted to extricate himself, he triggered a small avalanche that picked him up and flung him against a rock head first. Helen tried to move to him and was overwhelmed herself and buried.

"Hang on," Jacques yelled to everyone left. "Let it play out!"

When the snow stopped sliding down, he began moving toward Helen, half wading, half swimming through the snow. The footing was treacherous—he found he made the best progress by lying down on the snow and pushing against the rocks with his feet while doing something like a butterfly stroke with his hands until he got to where he thought Helen lay.

Meanwhile, Collette mimicked him in an effort to reach Soob from the other side of the avalanche.

Helen was nowhere to be seen, so Jacques felt around with his feet.

Something, or someone grabbed his leg and started climbing up him. Jacques cried out in startlement before he realized it had to be Helen. He reached down into the snow, found a hand, and pulled her up. Her face was ashen white, and she coughed in great hacking spasms that gradually decreased in frequency and harshness.

"Don't try breathing snow," she choked out as the coughs subsided.

"Can you make it out?" Jacques asked.

"What about Soob?" Helen asked, followed by another fit of coughing.

"We're looking. I'm not sure when this will let go again." Jacques tossed his head in the direction of the snow pile. "I don't want to lose all of us."

"Yeah. Okay."

"Watch your step."

She nodded and began to pick her way out of the avalanche area.

Jacques resumed "swimming" toward where he thought Soob's last position was. Despite the cold of the snow, he was sweating with effort. Soon, he and Collette met in the middle without having found Soob.

"It may have carried him downhill a ways," Collette said. "Let's stay in contact so we don't miss anything."

They did, slowly feeling their way through the snow shoulder to shoulder, foothold by foothold, steadying each other when the other slipped.

"Jacques!" Collette said at last. "I don't think this is a rock."

Quickly, they dug down with their hands and found the still form of their comrade. They brushed the snow away from his head with their bare hands. He had bled from a scalp wound, but not, it seemed, profusely. Collette tried to take his pulse and shook her head.

"Get him free first," Doc called. "The cold may reduce his life signs. We're trying to make a smooth area for him to lie down, clear of the avalanche danger."

"Yes," Jacques said, and bent to the task of extricating Soob's limp, motionless body.

In one gravity, it would have been impossible, but the gentle pull of Cube World made them supermen and superwomen. Jacques and Collette finally freed him and built a ramp of compressed snow to pull him up to the surface. There, they dragged him, as if he were a toboggan, toward the edge of the avalanche. Doc and an apparently recovered Helen took over then as Jacques and Collette collapsed in the snow in exhaustion.

"The good news," Doc proclaimed at length, "is that he isn't dead. Unfortunately, that may be the bad news as well. I wish I had the resources of a hospital..."

∞◊∞

Two days later, they were near the end of their food. Soob was still unconscious and, though they'd managed to get some water into him, they had no IV or liquid nourishment. He could, Jacques realized, be the first to starve to death.

"It's got to be apastron," Helen said. "The weather should start to moderate. Half rations may give us four days. We could just go hungry for another five or six. Spring should come quickly."

"Not quickly enough for Soob, I fear," Doc replied.

"I think we need to try again," Collette said. "Try smarter."

Jacques reviewed events in his mind. "I could try to trigger another avalanche."

"Risky," Doc said.

"Yeah. I'll need some kind of head gear, and a long tether. If I get buried, pull me out."

That was greeted with silence. Everyone realized the risk involved. But they were not going to sacrifice one of their own. One for all, all for one, Jacques thought. The beau geste. The stuff of legends. He looked around and everyone nodded.

They had one log left—in a small blessing, they'd needed less fire to keep warm than initially anticipated. Jacques planned to use it to put some distance between himself and what he thought would be the most unstable snow.

They planned it like a military campaign, beating a packed snow path between rocks to the target area. With a rope around his waist, Jacques advanced. As he approached the center, however, the path gave way, and he found his boot in water. Apparently, a melt creek was forming beneath the snow.

He extricated himself, made a "dry" snow path around the hole and trudged on.

Then he was there. He made his way up the snow as high as he could, then used the log to bludgeon the snow above him. Nothing. He whacked it again with similar results, then he pushed the log into the snow and tried to lever some out of the pile. He was doing this again when Colette shouted.

"Jacques, above you! Look out!"

He glanced up the snow hill and saw the avalanche coming. He backed off as quickly as he could without abandoning the log–they would need it for fuel–and avoided the worst of the oncoming snow. The tether, pulled by all his companions, moved him out of the deluge.

When things settled down, there was a gap above the snow hill and the skylight, filled only by the rope they had left a couple of weeks earlier. And above that was daylight.

They tested the rope with their total weight and found it had not gone rotten. Climbing it in the low local gravity was no problem and soon Jacques and Doc reached the snowy surface. Doc, whose voice carried farther, yelled down the hole to let them know they were out. Then they put on improvised snowshoes and headed for the forest.

The landscape had been transformed; snow weighed much less here than on an Earth-gravity world and compressed much less under its own weight. Drifts towered around them, and the lava tube had been a ridge to start with.

As they neared the forest, they noticed the snow under the trees pockmarked with holes about a hand's width wide.

"Somebody's out of hibernation, I think," Doc said.

"Somebody edible, I hope," Jacques answered. He had put hunger out of his mind, but with the prospect of food nearby, he felt almost irrationally famished.

With a whoosh, the something fell by Jacques, nearly hitting him on the head, punched a hole deep in the soft snow and stopped with a sort of distant plopping sound. He looked up just in time to avoid getting hit by the next one.

"Bitterwood fruit, high altitude version," Doc said, looking up.

"Hard to find down there," Jacques said, looking down the hole, hungry.

"Keep looking up," Doc said. "Come on now..."

He didn't have to wait long; a faint crack and rustle and shuffled under the next one before it completed its 300 meter fall. With the expertise of an American-rules football receiver he plucked it out of the sky before it hit the snow. Wordlessly, they split it, cleaned it and ate it immediately.

"Not too much more, right away," Doc said.

Jacques nodded. They caught a dozen more and headed back to the cave, somewhat lightheaded. They had survived the apastron winter and could get back to the business of finding the shuttle, or establishing a settlement.

∞◊∞

Doc rigged a tube from the shells of hirachnoid legs and some of their precious tape to get soup into Soob's stomach. They took turns watching him, feeding him, cleaning him, and finally, a week after the accident, he began to regain consciousness. But he wasn't really lucid and couldn't care for himself.

The snow melted and their sun was approaching its maximum size.

Temperatures climbed above freezing all day, snow melted, and the forest filled with bizarre critters and alien fragrances, as their sun approached.

Three days before periastron, they experienced a small earthquake, a thud followed by rumbling and groaning for about twenty seconds. Stones rocked around them, but nothing fell from the ceiling.

The next day, it hit 15 Celsius, and Helen went for a short swim in a small lake near the terrace edge. There were no other takers, but her joy in being bare and wet again, temperature be damned, made them all feel a bit warmer. They had a picnic in front of a low concave ridge of bare red rock by the lakeshore that sheltered them from the breeze and reflected the feeble sunlight on them. It was pleasant—even warm—there.

Helen picked up a rock and showed it to Jacques. "Geologically speaking," she said, "we're on a lava field between two volcanoes. I'll bet it slides down over millions of years and subducts just beyond the edge of the ocean."

"Then gets recirculated?" Doc asked.

Helen nodded. "I expect so, if this configuration is more or less stable over eons."

"What powers it?" Doc asked. "A world this small should lose heat faster than radioisotopes make it."

"Tides, maybe." Helen shrugged. "I wish I could do a simulation."

"There needs to be another world, further out, to keep the orbit eccentric," Doc offered. "A Neptune-mass giant, maybe."

"We haven't seen one," Collette said. "I think we would have."

Jacques nodded. "That's true, though I haven't looked carefully."

Helen said, "It might be dimmer than you think. Given the air pressure and temperature, I'm thinking we get half or something less of solar insolation here. But the primary is an M dwarf, so the visual light is maybe a tenth... half of a tenth... the amount of visual light one gets on Earth, and maybe a sixteenth of that at the nearest plausible giant planet orbit."

Jacques agreed. "Yes. A Jupiter equivalent would be something like an eightieth as bright. That's third or fourth magnitude here–visible but not really noticeable."

"Or," Doc said, "the planet could be closer to the star and too hard to see in the twilight."

Another, lesser quake interrupted the discussion.

"We can't stay forever," Jacques said, voicing what they all thought, staring up at the lava tube ceiling. "We're apparently still some distance from the shuttle. The season is getting on."

"We're about 48 kilometers above sea level now," Helen said. "I'm not sure it would be wise to winter at any higher altitude. What we could do is lay out supply caches at higher altitudes this summer, then make a dash up the following year."

"I should stay with Soob," Doc said.

"We should have two able bodied people here," Jacques countered.

"We can rotate placing the caches," Collette offered. "You and me, Helen and me... you and Helen."

Did she sound just a bit hesitant about the last pairing? Jacques wondered. Helen's approach to the three men, two women thing, was to spread her attention around more or less equally. Collette had not really tried to keep up; though she had genuine affection for Soob and Doc, she had taken a proprietary interest in Jacques. This flattered and excited Jacques, but the long term implications also worried him. Taking care of human needs was important, he thought, but in their present circumstances "keeping it professional" might be the best policy. Helen was having none of that, of course. Still, he had no complaints from others. The discussion went on to the more comfortable subject of logistics and schedule.

The result of all this was that, on what he had determined to be periastron, midsummer's day, he and Collette set out, loaded up with as much as they could carry.

# CHAPTER 14
# JACOB'S LADDER

Up and down, up and down the crews went. They could go up three terraces and back in a day, and it generally took two trips to set enough supplies for a trip to a higher stage–though on the first two stages, they found they could stretch things by foraging. As summer drew to a close, they reached the tree line at 48 kilometers altitude, where it was only above freezing for a few hours a day. A hardy form of tanglegrass kept on over the next three terraces, and this was grazed on by a four-footed relative of the kangasaur about six times the size of an African elephant. It didn't have a prehensile nose, though, and made do with only one flat tusk growing from the lower jaw and a talented tongue.

These were far too big to think about killing, but the "hairadactyls" that tended them were another matter. These were eagle-sized and pigeon-brained, so the staging crews came back with as much as they took up.

The terraces changed; the higher ones were no longer sheer cliffs, but more rounded and slumped, often with natural ramps on which herds had beaten paths from one level to another. Climbing cliffs became easier, but to make up for that, the slopes between them became steeper.

With the first chill of winter in the air, Jacques and Helen set out for the last foray until the next summer. They passed five depots, at 56, 60, 64, 68, and 72 kilometers altitude–as estimated from the wrist comp's barometric readings–on the way up, overnighting in a tiny log lean-to on permafrost. They established a depot at 76 kilometers in a small cave on a rare outcropping of rock in a field of ice. By 83 kilometers the ice was gone; they'd found a small lava tube, however, and the rock below it was still warm. Wrapped in their batskin sleeping rolls, with a tiny fire guarding the entrance, Jacques felt downright cozy.

"What do you think?" Helen asked. "Only thirteen kilometers up to the one bar level." She snuggled up to him, as natural and unconcerned as ever.

On Earth, Jacques thought, thirteen kilometers altitude gain would be ridiculous for an up and back. But with the gravity being only about an eighth of Earth's at this altitude, and the terrain now simply rolling hills paved with smooth pahoehoe lava, it was probably doable.

"The oxygen partial pressure is going down," Jacques said. "It's harder to start a fire. We're still above Earth normal pressure, about 1,200 millibars, but oxygen partial pressure must be less than Earth's."

"Time to put the shipsuits on?" she asked.

Jacques thought about it. Their carefully preserved shipsuits had hoods, transparent in front, that could be sealed air tight. They were intended to serve as emergency vacuum suits on spacecraft. They could easily hold a few hundred millibars of pressure differential. They used the heat of their wearers' bodies to power the efficient nanosystems that removed carbon dioxide, but...

"They still need an air supply, and we don't have one. Maybe we can rig up some kind of bellows for next year. But we can wear them for warmth tomorrow, along with our batskins."

"Our Cube World language is evolving."

"Huh?"

Helen laughed. "You dropped the 'mega.' So I'm wearing 'batskins.' It's a better word."

"Yeah. If Gabe and company have made a similar discovery, they'll call it dragonskin, or something like that. Then we'll argue about it."

"If we ever see them again. Or maybe if our descendants meet theirs."

He tried to envision some future Cube World with two independent cultures, not speaking the same language, not having the same values, possibly even going to war with each other. The prospect made him shudder.

"No descendants. No. We're leaving this place. We're going to recover our technology, get robots working, make spaceships and a starship and go home."

"That's a long term dream," Helen said. "In the mean time, we need to settle in, build a town with enough room in it for children. We don't have robots, at least not yet. So we need more people." She grinned at him. "I've never been pregnant before. I'm looking forward to it."

He looked at her in abject horror. "With Soob down, we can't afford to have another person disabled."

She shook her head. "Then we'd best get on with it now before we lose someone else. I don't want to spend eternity being the last person on this planet. Yes, I've opened my tubes and I'm giving it my best shot."

"You're making a big decision for all of us."

She nodded and smiled cheerfully. "I didn't think I'd win a vote. You want to kick me off the planet? It's my body."

"You're not already..."

"Could even be yours. It's hard to tell just yet." She snuggled up to him. "Don't worry. I can't get more pregnant."

"Hey, if you aren't I don't want to..." he said.

But she sealed his mouth with a kiss, and biology took over.

Afterwards, as afterglow faded into sleep, he wondered about man's ability to rationalize in the face of a determined womanly assault. Helen, he realized, was probably in charge here, preferring to lead from behind him, almost as Collette thought Leo might have led Gabe. In an era of genetic engineering leveling, she was still clearly smarter than anyone else in their small team, but her sexuality made some people forget her mind. She was Helen Athena, all powerful, leading him on, enticing him. Then she became Collette and they lay down together. Then Collette became Ascendant Chryse and they decided to make babies and fill this planet with them. Then they could outvote Gabe Eddie and Leo. They needed to do it quickly before Leo stopped them.

Helen woke him up with a kiss before the dream reached its climax.

"Time to get going."

∞◇∞

They had their tiny camp packed before sunrise and set out upward under starlight, probing ahead of themselves with their flute plant walking sticks.

Antares alone provided enough light for them to find their way.

"It's much brighter than Venus, up here," Helen said. "I'd say about minus sixth magnitude."

"Hmm, maybe brighter than that. Almost like a crescent moon. I'll give it minus seven."

"Maybe. Let's say that's a maximum. Split the difference; since it's something like first magnitude from Earth, that would put it about 7.5 magnitudes, or a factor of 1000 brighter than from Earth. So it's thirty-some times closer, at least. Only five parsecs or so."

"About the same distance between 36 Ophiuchi and Earth," Jacques said. "You can barely see 36 Ophiuchi at that distance; this star casts shadows."

"I wonder what happens here when it goes supernova."

"Whoever built this place may have taken that into consideration," Jacques said, struggling to keep his mind on putting one synapse in front of the next. "Maybe they've predicted the date."

The terraces were gone, along with any hint of water. The lava field looked flat, except that they were bent over at almost forty five degrees to the surface. Part of that was the slope of the mountain to the gravitational field, and part of it was the wind they were slogging into. It was dry and cold, but Jacques thought it might change as day came. Footing was treacherous; the lava was covered with a loose grit that could slide underfoot, and thin spots in the lava could give way without warning, leaving one's foot dangling in a lava tube.

That said, they were able to maintain a fairly brisk pace without their packs, about three meters a second, Jacques thought. We're putting some distance behind us. He looked back over the featureless landscape, and realized he couldn't recognize anything.

"Whoa, Helen. I can't see our camp!"

"Can you see the horizon against the mist?"

"Okay. Yes, I can see it. The bulge."

"If we've been headed directly uphill, the camp should be just below the bulge. We haven't gone too far to find it again, I think. But we should build a cairn here. A big one.

It was easier said than done. Portable rocks were hard to find in a pahoehoe field, but by stomping around they were able to collapse a small lava tube and use the pieces of its roof to build an upright pillar. 'Upright' proved to be about thirty degrees to the local slope, so they called it "the leaning tower of pieces."

They found they would hike upward for about an hour before it became hard to see a cairn, so that became their routine. As dawn came, they could see farther, but could also see better and move faster, so the hour interval remained about the same. Six cairns and an hour into the trip, they realized the ground was getting warm. An incongruous cloud lay ahead of them.

"Jacques, I don't think we should try to build a cairn here," Helen said. "Look."

He turned to where she pointed and saw a piece of lava fall with a crunch into a new hole. A river of brilliant orange light shone through it.

They went quickly right until the steam cloud was no longer in front of them, and the ground seemed cooler to the touch. Some experimental stomping found them shards for the cairn.

Jacques found he was a little short on breath, and hooked his wrist comp to the solar array. The air near the lava surface was about zero C, but if he held the wrist comp high over his head, it recorded minus twenty-five. Atmospheric pressure was down to 998 millibars.

"Up ahead... I think the lava field stops beyond that ridge."

Jacques saw, and nodded. "I don't think we can go too much farther..." he stopped to breathe deeply..."without more oxygen. I'd guess we're getting about half what we should, partial pressure around a hundred millibars."

Helen nodded. "Just a little farther. I want to see where the lava comes from."

They pushed on for another thirty minutes and arrived at the ridge. Above the lava was a smooth band of material that looked vaguely like concrete. Beyond that, uphill was a featureless plane of gray. He boosted Helen up over the "concrete" and she pulled him up afterward. It was absolutely flat.

"Is the shuttle still there?" Helen asked.

Jacques checked. "Yes, it has a somewhat stronger signal, but... The reading was coming from directly in front of him, but he was standing at about a thirty degree angle, which meant that the signal was coming from below Cube World's surface. "It's below us, Helen. Ahead and somehow below—a radio propagation trick?"

"I'm not sure, but I wouldn't think so." She pulled out the binoculars and scanned the horizon. "I can't see anything here. Maybe it's on the other side of the ridge. On the other face."

"How far to the ridge, do you think?" Jacques asked.

"Maybe a thousand kilometers. At five kilometers an hour, maybe two hundred hours."

"A week. We'd need enough oxygen for a week."

"Next year, if we can figure out how to store it," Helen said. "I want to stand on the ridge and look at both faces."

"While breastfeeding?" Jacques quipped, and instantly regretted it.

But Helen just laughed. "There will be time."

"Time to go home now."

He saw it out of the corner of his eye when he turned around to retrace their steps. It was just a bump in the otherwise geometrically smooth curve of the lava source ridge, an indeterminate distance away.

"Binoculars, Helen. Over there—a bump on the lava source ridge."

She pulled the binoculars from her belly kit, plugged them into the solar array and sighted in on it. "It looks like a shelf sticking out of the plain. The top is probably level, gravitationally, the front, vertical. Like a dormer window. Four and a fraction klicks distant."

"We should go for it. It probably has something to do with this place." He stomped his foot on the surface for emphasis, and almost lost his footing on the slope.

"We'd be finding our way home in the dark."

"We left that way."

They stared at each other. It was clearly more of a risk than Helen wanted, but Jacques weighed that against the potential for a breakthrough. It was a discovery that emphasized the differences in their attitudes; Helen for accepting a long stay and adapting to the world, Jacques putting almost all of his efforts into finding a way out.

"Okay," Helen said at length. "But let's go down to the lava source ridge—it's almost level on top—easier to walk on. It looks like the front of the structure is just a few meters back from the ridge."

They reached the structure well past local noon, but Jacques figured they still had seven hours plus twilight to return and find their camp. Helen was nervous and he had picked up the pace as much as his oxygen starved lungs would let him. The structure proved large—

maybe twenty meters tall in front—and featureless as they approached from the side. But when they got to the front they saw a huge black rectangle, about twenty meters by ten in the wall in front of them.

"I'd say it's a door," Helen said in wonderment. "A great big garage door."

They got a greater shock as they approached and it opened by simply vanishing.

# CHAPTER 15
# BEHIND THE CURTAIN

"**A**nd there we were," Helen told the assembled group, "inside this enormous, enormous room with great curving arches, huge pillars–of solid diamond, I'd guess–catwalks the width of airplane runways, huge machines rolling around without making any sound whatsoever."

"It was lit inside?" Collette asked.

Jacques nodded. "There were point sources every few kilometers, I'd guess. They looked like stars, but much brighter. In the distance they kind of merged into a general glow. We only took half an hour inside–it was too cold to stay overnight and we had to get back to camp. But it looks like there's a road through to the other side of the ridge. Which is where my readings indicate the shuttle is."

He looked around the group. Soob nodded and smiled at him; he wasn't able to speak or walk without assistance, but at least the higher functions of his mind hadn't been too badly damaged by his near suffocation. Doc said he was getting better every day.

If they had all been healthy, they might have tried for the other side immediately, but they didn't want to do that with only two people, gone into an unknown environment for the entire winter, and they couldn't bring Soob in his present state. So Eagles Nest was getting ready for their second winter. Provisions were piled high in the ice-cave. Partitions of flute plant mats broke the wind through the cave and gave them private bedrooms.

"Did anyone, or anything, notice you were there?" Collette asked. "Seems like pretty loose security to me."

"Whatever guards the door apparently didn't see us as a threat," Jacques said. "The way it just vanished... and it was solid before. I touched it."

"It could be some form of programmable matter," Helen said. "People have been working on it for forever. Send it one signal and it's a solid wall, send it another and it's just dust in the air."

"Which we breathed," Jacques added, "without, apparently, any ill effects."

"So you have alien nanites running around inside you," Doc concluded.

Soob grunted, and reached for his slate, wrote, and handed the slate to Collette.

"All of us since arrival. Place is managed!" she read.

"Okay," Helen said in a loud voice. "Whoever you are, you can stop playing with us. We have better things to do with our lives."

There was, of course, no response, and the group had a nervous laugh.

∞◊∞

The winter passed, if not comfortably, with much less difficulty. They had enough food. Jacques rigged a system to keep the top entrance open, and they even managed a few trips to the first two stage camps, bringing more provisions and creating more living room.

On one trip, they saw a megabat crash into the snow. Why it did so, they couldn't guess, but its carcass yielded a fresh supply of batskin and more meat than they could eat in years. What they brought back to the cave with them became frozen steaks and jerky for next summer's expedition.

Finally the snow melted and Jacques finished his carved stone marker, following their names with: Eagles Nest. Days 72-195

They had to travel light, of course, and left countless things they had made over the two winters. They told themselves they would be back again someday, knowing it would be unlikely. They imagined tourists going through their cave in some ten thousand years, looking at their carvings, primitive furniture, stone kitchenware, and all.

Helen had tears in her eyes as she left. She had hoped to raise a child there. Soob touched her arm. He walked well enough, now, but still could not talk. What memories Eagles Nest must have for him? But with last looks back, they were on their way, with full packs, along a now well-beaten trail to Tree Line Camp.

∞◇∞

They reached the maintenance entrance a week later, quite prepared for it to not open for them. But it did, and in they went, with Collette, Doc and Soob making appropriate sounds of wonder at the network of roadways, braces and catwalks between great vertical tubes that climbed from far below to far above. Here and there, Jacques thought he could see robots moving around on huge catwalks on the inside of the mountain surface, many kilometers away. The place was obviously being actively maintained.

They had, nominally, forty days provisions with them; Jacques thought two weeks would get them through the 1000 kilometers to the other side. If they found no exit at the other end, they could conceivably retrace their steps on short rations. Shortcut though it might be, it was a long, cold, hard walk through a complete desert. There was nothing to be done about disguising their presence and they had to litter the clean roadway with hirachnoid limb shells and worse.

On the flat, hard surface, however, they found they could half walk, half jog in a kind of long loping stride that saved their feet and ate up the kilometers. They took turns holding Soob's hand—his legs were strong enough but his coordination wasn't fully back yet. It was a bit embarrassing for him, but he bore it with good grace. Going by the increase in signal strength, they managed between 61 and 72 kilometers the first day, and between 55 and 67, the second.

On the first break of the third day, Helen announced, "We're going downhill!"

They all looked at her. The road had seemed level when they started, but now—though it was hard to tell in the low gravity—they, indeed, seemed to be leaning back a bit.

Jacques kicked himself mentally for not having seen that sooner.

Doc groaned. "Of course, of course. This is a brace as well as a road. To be in compression—not supported by the vertical members, it has to come closer to the planet at its center than the ends—as an interior buttress, it's almost straight."

"Downhill!" Collette exclaimed, "Then we'll need to push it a little more now to compensate for being slower later on. But we'll get more oxygen as we go lower."

So they took to loping a little faster–almost a low-gravity jog–and covered around 80 kilometers in two seven-hour sessions that day. The next day was close to 80 kilometers as well, but the apparent downward slope gradually lessened and by the fifth day they were more or less level and probably approaching the lowest point of the road. From then on, it would be uphill.

Soob's balance was improving every day, and by the time they started going uphill, he'd felt comfortable without a hand holder, though he kept his flute plant walking stick.

They made camp on the fifth day on the road, in good spirits. They each carried a double-thickness batskin sack. With the short fur on the inside, these kept them warm and comfortable.

On the sixth day, they noted their road was joined on the right from below by an arch, the top of which was another road.

"That looks like a constant-radius road," Helen said, "with its own support system. It's not hanging from a shell support column. It would be nice to avoid the climb and end up somewhere that wasn't an Antarctic dry valley."

Collette shook her head. "How would we get to the surface? It's covered with rock. We'd be risking too much."

They were about to give up when Jacques remembered the network of catwalks just under the surface that he'd seen when they entered. "If we can't get out, we can climb up on the inside. We'll have saved enough time for it, I think."

"Just barely," Helen said. "We'd be putting our contingency plan in jeopardy."

"But if it works," Doc said, "we'd save several days and end up where we can forage. We'd be in much better shape."

"The shuttle is powered and active," Jacques said. "We must assume someone is using it. We must also assume that someone saw us go in the mountain. If we come out at a different altitude, that could be a surprise. It could be our only advantage."

"We were put here by an ideology-blinded fanatic," Collette said. "The bad guys aren't usually geniuses–we need to be wary, but let's not fail to give them a chance to make a mistake."

"I think we should give it a shot. What do you think, Soob?" Doc asked.

Their hunter smiled and pointed down the curved path.

∞◇∞

Longer and gravitationally level, it took them six days to traverse the constant radius path. It ended in a T intersection with a straight catwalk, four meters wide, on the inside surface of the mountain. Jacques could see nothing that looked like an entrance.

Soob grunted, and pointed above them. A tube hung down from the inside surface of the mountain, like a stalactite, with what looked like a flat, black circular face. It was about ten meters above them, and there was no ladder. A robot on top of one of the big machines that rolled around the catwalks wouldn't need one, of course.

So near yet so far, Jacques thought. But then he spotted an interior catwalk passing near the upper end of the tube.

Jacques imagined a line running from that catwalk to their catwalk at just the right angle to touch the tip of the downward projecting tube. He quickly explained what he had in mind to the group. They had two long lines, and tied them end to end. Jacques found a brace that led to the upper catwalk, and pulled himself up, hand over hand, careful not to look down until he was securely on the walkway. There were no rails, of course, for infallible machines.

But the catwalk had to be supported. He found a brace projecting from the inside surface of the mountain and managed to loop the line around that, then threw the other end down to Collette. She walked the end of the line along the lower catwalk until the middle of the line touched the end of the projecting tube. Secured with a loop of tanglegrass rope, Jacques wrapped his legs around the line and eased himself down, sloth style, until he was below the tube.

It was about a meter wide, and remained resolutely closed. He put a hand on it and pushed. Solid. Just for the hell of it, he shouted "Open!" at it. That did nothing.

Something had to make it open. The other door had responded to their presence, not some external computer demand. That bespoke of a distributed, semi-autonomous systems approach to Cube World–far more efficient and robust than a top-down control pyramid. The door opening trigger should be local.

Maybe they would have to wait for a maintenance robot to roll by. That could be a long time–things seemed to last in here. Or maybe they could simulate one.

"Everyone!" he shouted. "I want you to walk directly beneath me and jump up and down. I'm hoping there's a mass or weight sensor on the catwalk."

"Say again," was Collette's distant response.

He yelled again, louder, and got an okay back. The group walked beneath him, and, in a surreal sort of dance, jumped up and down in time. Nothing happened.

In frustration he slammed the palm of his hand at the surface above him.

And it vanished, rewarding his effort with a shower of dust. There was a circular shelf a few centimeters wide around the opening. He grabbed that with one hand and held on, hoping that would keep the door open, and then pulled his head inside. Inside the tube was a robust skeleton of truss work and tracks; apparently some fairly heavy equipment could use this passage. Boring machines? If so, he hoped they had done their job.

"I'm in!" he shouted down to the rest of the party. He used a length of green twine to tie his line securely to the inner framework of the tube. In the low gravity, the rest of the group would be able to pull themselves up, hand over hand. But first he needed to make sure there was an exit. "I'm going to see if there's a way out." He estimated the length of the tube. "I'll be back in about an hour."

Jacques climbed up the inner bracing of the tube. Up and up, he went, mostly by feel. Just before he thought he would need to drop back to the opening to make his self-imposed deadline, he emerged in what appeared to be a lava tube cave, not unlike the one they'd used for Eagles Nest. He could feel a slight breeze and smell fresh air.

∞◇∞

The cave exit proved to be a three-kilometer scramble over rocks in the dark. About halfway, they encountered a stream and a hundred meters or so down from that, enough dry silt that they could lie down. With nobody making an objection, they simply made camp there and slept for twelve and a half hours. Feeling optimistic, they decided to make breakfast double rations, and didn't start out again until they all felt ready.

Helen was in the lead as they reached the mouth of the cave. She scrambled over some rocks that partly blocked the exit and vanished from Jacques' view.

"Oh my God!" she yelled from somewhere outside. "They're alive!"

# CHAPTER 16
# THE OTHER SIDE OF THE
# MOUNTAIN

Everyone else started forward, but Collette held them back. "Weapons," she said. "Whatever we have."

Jacques and Collette strung their bows while Soob and Doc pulled the covers off their spears.

"Helen," Jacques yelled, "are you okay?"

There was a pause. "Yes. No danger so far. I don't think they've noticed me." The last was choked out in kind of an hysterical giggle.

The rest of the party climbed out, one by one. Little rock was visible in a forest of plants that had stems like blackwood trees but had huge, fleshy, triangular yellow leaves. Over them, a sparse canopy of trees of some unimaginable height dominated the landscape. Some of these were vaguely palm-like while others seemed to be more stalk-like, with only a hint of foliage around the upper stem. They were spaced far apart in the near field but merged in the distance to look like a solid line of wood. They swayed in the soft breeze.

Rather, some of them swayed, mainly the ones absent luxuriant palm-like crowns.

"Oh my God!" Collette echoed Helen.

"I don't think that's possible," Helen said. "Even as I see it, it can't be? The heat rejection problem...."

Confused, Jacques scanned around at the distant waving stalks and watched one of them touch the crown of a leafy tree and, apparently, come away with some of the leaves. A sense of disquiet rose within him. Plants feeding on other plants?

He scrambled up higher on the rocks of the cave mouth to where he could see down slope over three terraces, a distance of about eleven kilometers, at least, on the other side of the ridge. If that held here—he was looking at trees almost two hundred meters tall.

He craned his head up to find one of the nearer stalk trees and started to follow it down.

It moved as he did so, not swaying, but moving laterally with slow, infinite patience. A massive leg swung ponderously clear of undergrowth forest, tall as any of the triangle leaf trees.

"Oh my God!" he said.

The beast, for that was what it was, moved with what seemed a glacial pace, an illusion of scale, he realized. It may have taken seven seconds for that leg to swing forward, but the footprints would be something like eighty meters apart. He could not have outrun it. The foot set down gently, not thunderously.

"Its head must be 160 meters high," Jacques said, a touch of awe in his voice.

"I'm not sure it's a head," Doc answered. "It may be more like a trunk with sense organs. I think that bulge above the shoulders is more likely the true head."

The skin on the creature's sides seemed loosely hung, as if it was overlapping drapery. As it moved, there was a whooshing sound Jacques could hear, even a third of a kilometer or so away.

"It has gills?" Helen said softly, in wonder.

"Exhaust," Doc said. "It's about eight times the dimension of a large sauropod dinosaur from Earth's past. Everything else being more or less to scale, it would have some 500 times as much volume and mass, but only..." he laughed at the irony of 'only,' "...about sixty-some times the surface area with which to reject heat. It must blow a tremendous volume of air through itself with every step."

Soob scratched on his slate and gave it to Helen.

*Don't/do want see what eats it.*

Finding what *they* could eat was the first order of business. Nothing looked familiar to Jacques, or rather some of it did; the grasses were uncannily terrestrial-looking. The triangle-leaf trees had a pulpy pumpkin-sized fruit that was either out of reach, or hit the ground with a forceful splat even in the low gravity. They found a bamboo-like middle canopy plant; young shoots were an acceptable substitute for flute plant, but the fern-like fronds were inedible. In sunny patches of ground, they found a low plant with leaves shaped like pentagonal snowflakes.

Making a virtue of necessity, Doc made a kind of pudding of fall-mashed triangle-leaf tree fruit. It proved to be a good diuretic. Cooking it didn't improve matters.

The white part of the grass roots could be nibbled, but it would take a huge amount of grass to make a meal. None of the leaves would stay down.

"We're just damned lucky we haven't seriously poisoned ourselves," Doc said on the morning of the third day. We need to think about going back."

"We'll be starved by the time we get there," Jacques said.

Doc nodded. "Uncomfortable to be sure, but we should survive. Another day or two, and one or more of us might not make it."

"We can try for the shuttle now," Jacques said. "At least take time to get a fix. It may be near."

The shuttle, if they could gain control of it, would solve the food problem. But taking any time away from exploratory foraging now could put them in severe difficulty later.

Soob wrote: "Go for it."

"Come on, Collette, let's find some food," Helen said.

Doc patted Jacques on the back and went with them.

Jacques and Soob found a gap in the tree cover where sunlight fell and set up the solar cells and plugged in. The shuttle signal was very strong. He looked around, and saw trees and a few "dinotowers."

"It's around here somewhere, Soob. Maybe we can get one of those guys to tell us," he joked, pointing at a dinotower a few hundred meters away.

Soob nodded, seriously it seemed, and motioned to Jacques that he wanted to go to the dinotower. Soon they were at the rear leg of one of the monsters. Soob tried to climb it, but the thick skin proved impossible to grip.

Jacques went to the tail and back along it until he reached where it rested on the ground. It was as thick as he was tall, but with measured jump, he was able to land on top of it. Soob followed him. They began walking up the giant's back; its head was actually lost in a low mist.

"I hope it doesn't decide to swat a fly, just now," he said back to Soob.

Soob gestured for him to keep moving, faster, and Jacques picked up the pace.

The huge body moved under them as they reached its hips and they fell, spread-eagled on its rump. Jacques looked over to Soob, who looked back at him, wide-eyed. He pointed to something behind Jacques.

Jacques turned and saw a huge head descending from the mist. It was vaguely frog-like, and almost two meters wide, with eyes as big as basketballs, and a small central crest. As it came toward him, the mouth opened, revealing broad, sharp teeth that looked like human incisors as much as anything.

He thought about jumping, but they were too high—even in the low gravity, the fall would lead to serious injury. He tried waving at it.

"Hi."

The head stopped. He could see the long neck now, the mists were clearing. The huge eyes focused on him. Scale matters, Jacques thought. While the head in front of him was a ridiculously tiny part of the dinotower's bulk, it probably contained a brain several times the size of the one on his shoulders.

Jacques tried to pantomime looking. Soob got up and joined him. The creature watched them for a while, then laid its head on its back in front of them.

"I think," Jacques said, with more than a little awe in his voice, "that we're being offered a ride."

He and Soob hopped up on the broad, flat head and hung onto the narrow crest as the dinotower's head whooshed back up through the mist to its usual height.

Then, with a gentle rocking motion, the beast began to move out toward the edge of the terrace, about as fast as a man could run, in Jacques' estimation. In the denser Cube World air, this made for a significant wind of passage, and he had to hang on tightly.

They hadn't gone far when the head began to drop down through the mists again, down and down, like a huge, fast elevator. Suddenly, in front of them, about fifty meters through the trees, was the shuttle.

"It must have seen men before, with it. It's putting us back where we belong," Jacques said.

The head reached ground, and they hopped off. For a moment, human and dinotower stared at each other, then the dinotower raised its head through the clouds and began to glide back to its feeding ground.

Jacques turned his attention to the shuttle, a big, blunt upside down ice-cream cone, its gray lines blending in with the triangle-leaf tree trunks like it was designed to do so. Soob immediately gestured for him to get down. Of course. If they could see it, it could see them, and it probably had instructions of the kind not anticipated by its AI programmers. Jacques thought furiously. No, there was nothing to do but try contacting it and go from there. It would better be a collective decision, but there it was now and it might fly away. He touched the transmit icon on his wrist comp screen and began talking.

"This is Engineering Officer Jacques Song. We have..."

The shuttle sounded a warning tone.

"Duck! Now!" Jacques said, pushing Soob to the ground. "It's lifting off!"

With a roaring cascade of exhaust, the shuttle leaped skyward and was already hundreds of meters overhead and shrinking as the wave of hot air rolled over them.

Jacques stared up, helpless. Then he collapsed onto a log, and put his face in his hands, tears flowing freely. Everything over the last few months went by in his mind—the parrot beaked fish, the rescues, the split-up, the escape from the fire, the winter in the cave... all the work, all the effort. Gone. All his efforts fruitless, leaving them with the prospect of retreat, starvation, and living out their lives as savages.

Helen may think that worthwhile, Jacques thought. But he wasn't sure he did. He didn't think he could face an eternity of the kind of labor and striving it had taken them to survive for the last three months, and if he ended his existence now, there would be one less mouth to feed.

Soob was trying to get his attention, shoving his slate at him. With a groan, Jacques took it.

*Not out of range. Keep talking!!*

Jacques hurriedly turned back to the wrist comp, pointing its directional antenna at the tip of the ascending contrail, said everything he planned to say, and added, "We are at the end of our food supply. If you leave us you may be responsible for human deaths." If there was anything left of the higher functions in its AI, Jacques thought, that should do it.

The shuttle did not deviate from its upward path, and its contrail ended where it left the atmosphere.

Then Jacques looked down at his wrist comp screen. The "message received" telltale glowed. Pure automation, he supposed, but one microscopic step above complete hopelessness. At least he had the energy to trudge back to camp with Soob, following the swath cleared by the dinotower.

When they got there, Helen, Collette, and Doc all had big grins on their faces, and their arms filled with big thick roots of some kind. Presumably, that meant a respite from the starvation part of his bleak scenario. He wanted to go back into the cave and lie down and leave the explanations to Soob, but, of course, that was impossible. He decided on the short and sweet version.

"We found the shuttle. It flew away. I'm not feeling so good right now, I just..."

"Try some of this and you'll feel a lot better," Doc said, laughing.

"It's really... I can't describe. Just wow!" Collette said.

Despite the near freezing temperatures, Helen discarded her clothes and started dancing, holding a morsel of the root out to Jacques. "Come on, lover boy, cheer up," she said.

Collette was going after Soob, in a somewhat less spectacular, though equally determined manner.

Why not? Jacques thought. Why the hell not?

Because if they all went crazy, they would all die, not just him. He knocked the piece of root out of Helen's hand.

She looked confused. "Jacques, honey, it's all right. We're just a bit giddy. We're okay. We're due for a party."

"You're intoxicated. You're not thinking right," he said, suspecting that reason would be futile while they were under the influence of whatever it was.

Something went crunch in the nearby underbrush. Jacques turned and found himself facing what appeared to be a close cousin of Tyrannosaurus Rex, except it had a beak instead of teeth, and four tiny little arms instead of two.

It didn't seem to know what to make of them. He grabbed his flute plant staff.

"Soob, get everyone in the cave," he yelled, as he tossed his bag of electronics to the hunter and stood to face the beast.

Everyone was not going to the cave. Helen was behind him saying, "Hey, that's a big dinosaur, isn't it. Maybe it would like some candy. Give the dino some candy."

"What it would like is you," Jacques snapped. "But it isn't sure yet. Get in the cave!"

"You're no fun! Hey, Soob, where are you going with my roots? Come back here."

Jacques risked a quick look back. Soob had grabbed all the roots and was taking them into the cave. The other three, complaining, were going after him. Nothing wrong with that part of Soob's brain, Jacques thought.

The "tyrannoparrot" began rocking back and forth, looking at him and the people disappearing into the cave mouth. Why had it not attacked? Maybe, Jacques thought, with his staff, he looked approximately like something it hadn't seen yet that was dangerous, poisonous, or both. They must have stood there, tiny human staring down a three-story monster, for almost fifteen minutes. Then, abruptly, the tyrannoparrot turned and strode off into the forest.

He had a feeling of déjà vu about this, something he'd read or viewed. Lewis and Clark. One of them had faced down a grizzly bear in the middle of a river with a staff like his. Someday, he told himself, he should find out why the monster had spared him. But for now, it was interesting to note how the adrenaline had set aside his depression. When it came down to it, in spite of everything, he still very much wanted to live.

He joined Soob at the cave and they started a fire at the mouth. The other three had fallen into a deep sleep, so there were no protests as into the fire went the big thick tubers. The gentle breeze out of the cave mouth kept the fumes from going in, while Soob and he pulled shifts to keep the fire and their friends alive through the night.

∞◊∞

Jacques awoke to find Doc poking around the fire.

"Doc?" he said, fearing the worst. He put some more wood on the fire.

"We should have a sample," he said. "Imagine a raw potato, but already a little buttery. The drug affect didn't set in until half an hour after ingestion. I suspect it's a chemical given off by a bacteria-like bug and not the root itself."

He finally came up with a short segment of charred root and handed it to Jacques.

"Try a very small piece. We'd each eaten maybe a hundred grams, and if I'm right about the bacterium, the fire will have killed it and degraded the toxin. But, I'm not sure I trust myself."

Jacques held the charred morsel in his hand, feeling very uncertain.

"It is the only edible thing we've found here," Doc said, looking down at the ground. "we don't have much choice, and, by the way, thank you for saving my life again." He said the last in a whisper and with a slight bow.

Jacques touched him on the shoulder for a moment.

Then, with a wry smile, Jacques took a bite of the root, still warm from the fire. It did taste like buttered potatoes, and, irrationally, he wished for some salt. Or maybe not irrationally. They probably weren't getting quite enough salt. He swallowed and waited to go crazy.

"Half an hour, you say?"

Doc nodded.

Jacques unfolded their little solar array, plugged in the wrist comp, and sat down in front of the fire. "Do you remember what I said about the shuttle?"

"It flew away. I'm sorry I wasn't in a state of mind to appreciate that news, or, maybe I'm not so sorry. Pretty disappointing, that."

"Yeah."

Doc shivered and covered himself with his batskin sleep sack, even though the fire was going strong. "We'll need to move to a lower altitude for a permanent camp."

"Or go back to where we know the territory better."

Doc nodded. "A little easier, if cooking this root works."

They continued to talk until Collette, Soob and Helen joined them.

"I wish I didn't remember everything so well," was Helen's only comment.

"We need a name for this stuff," Collette said. "It should be a warning, like 'crazyroot'." "I'll go with crazyroot," Jacques said, "and, by the way, am I crazy yet?"

"We accidentally cooked some, and he's tried that," Doc explained.

"You sound okay to me, Jacques," Collette said.

Soob tried to talk. It came out something like, "Yuh uh," but those were his first words since almost suffocating in the snow drift.

Doc cut another piece off the cooked 'crazyroot' and popped it in his own mouth. "Okay. I think it would be best if Jacques and Soob gather the next batch. I don't want to be tempted. It felt good, way too good."

"We can't stay here," Helen said. "I mean the temptation would always be there."

She wasn't one to resist sensual temptations, Jacques thought. But at least she knew herself.

"I wouldn't want to raise children with that kind of temptation around, either," Collette said, "and I think the megabats are probably easier to deal with than the tyranno-parrots."

"There are four other faces on this cube that we haven't seen," Doc said. "It's probably premature to say which is best for us."

Soob grunted and tried to speak, then shook his head and pulled his slate from his shoulder bag and scratched, *R we welcome anywhere?*

Jacques thought about the huge maintenance operations in the hollow ridge behind him. This immense, self perpetuating operation had to be controlled by a high grade artificial intelligence.

"I think so. Of course, something is clearly in charge here. But it has made no effort to communicate, to wipe us out, nor to help us, at least as far as we can tell."

"Maybe it's not aware we're here, like you're not aware that specific microbe is on or in your body," Doc said. "Our impact, so far, could be well under its threshold."

"I don't know," Collette said. "If we made something to manage this, it would be very concerned with biological contamination."

Helen laughed. "We've become like Gabe. He knows there's a god, or at least says he does, but what does it want, what does it expect of him? When it doesn't say, he makes up answers, or quotes others who made up answers."

"Then that becomes doctrine, regardless of any later evidence," Collette said.

Doc chortled. "People like Gabe have evolved an ability to withstand a level of cognitive dissonance that would be fatal to ordinary mortals. We may make up answers, but we test them."

Soob scratched furiously on his slate. "People make this? 400 years."

Jacques shivered. Yes, a thousand years in time, but only six hundred or so in space; the *Resolution* could easily have been passed by human descendants during its long slowdown from relativistic velocities. Before they left, the potential of self-replicating robots to make megastructures in decades or even years had just begun to be used; the solar power stations of the interstellar transport complex, the Venus sunscreen, and the beginnings of the Mercury sphere. What could they do in this age?

"They may feel we aren't ready to handle the shock of what humanity has become," Helen said quietly. "They could be right."

Collette shook her head. "So they let us starve to death? That doesn't make sense. Anyway, we need some food." She began poking around the fire, apparently hoping to find some cooked crazyroot missed in earlier searches. "We'll also need weapons."

Jacques wondered what sort of weapon would deter a tyrannoparrot, but after reflection decided something would be better than nothing. They made long spears, sharpening the ends of the "neobamboo" with a diagonal cut and fire-hardening them. Then they set out.

A couple hours later, burdened with roots and almost back to the camp, Jacques thought he heard a distant hissing noise, something between a waterfall and an angry cat. It seemed to be coming above him. He looked around. They were too high and too cold for something like a megabat, he thought.

Helen was looking too. "The shuttle? Everyone, the shuttle is coming back!"

# CHAPTER 17
# LOST AND FOUND

"Captain Song," it said as they approached, "I have determined that you are correct. As senior surviving crew member, command devolves on you. It was necessary to preserve life, get confirmatory data, and preserve the ignorance of the unauthorized users to carry out one more scheduled supply run. The *Resolution* shuttle *Fortitude* is now under your command. I will need your assistance to recover much of my memory."

Jacques looked at the shuttle, then back to Helen and the others, dumbfounded. Less than a Cube World day ago, he had hit rock bottom, contemplating suicide. Now, he had apparently succeeded in everything. Oh, there was still a lot to do, decisions to be made, questions to ask and have answered. But with the shuttle's replicator, they could do everything they wanted.

"We'll be on that in a moment," he said, softly, then turned to the party, "I, I have a hard time believing this, but I think we're over the hill here."

"We can move to better quarters, anyway," Doc said.

As it sank in, Jacques found himself emotionally unprepared for success. It was as if all the stress of the last few months had spilled out and left him as empty as a deflated balloon. He collapsed onto a nearby log, eyes moistening. "I just want to go home. I want to go home."

"Jacques," Helen answered. "We can't. Home is a thousand years in the past, sixteen hundred counting travel time. Whatever the Solar System has become, it's not home anymore. That's only in memory."

She was right, of course. They had all signed up for what was to have been a significant hunk of time displacement to go on the initial mission, but that was tiny compared to what they now contemplated. She led the way to the shuttle lock. "Permission to board, Captain?"

∞◇∞

The shuttle had been hobbled. The wireless data links it used to communicate with its robots had been removed. Its primary memory slots had been vacated, except for one card; clearly a "Trojan card" inserted by the saboteur. What the saboteur apparently did not know, was that there was a backup executive agent program in the engineering node; a limited AI but with the basic security protocols and Asimovian restraints. Absent a higher authority, this had followed the primary, but Jacques' statements had created a conflict, eventually resolved in Jacques' favor.

The shuttle had been used by Gabriel Eddie, Leo Surretta, Arroya Montez, and Evgenie Malenkov. No surprise there, Jacques thought. Gabe and eleven others had been revived and assigned to shuttles by the ship before its final crash into Cube World's atmosphere. They were supposed to recover CSUs that survived atmospheric entry–but that mission had been postponed. The Shuttle *Fortitude* had come down on another face of Cube World. It had taken Gabe some time to discover Jacques' group–which he'd done from the air.

"According to the log, he'd only just arrived when we met him," Collette said. "The Robinson Crusoe get-up was a ruse."

Doc nodded. "When he found us, he kept the shuttle a secret; apparently seeing an opportunity to become the dictator of a new accidental colony. He knew there was no danger in staying at New Landing–no wonder he was so adamant."

"If he'd only just gotten there, he couldn't have killed Ascendant Chryse," Helen observed.

Jacques stated the obvious. "We're missing a lot of information."

After mining what data they could from the saboteur's card, Jacques replaced it with a set of backup cards, in storage since before the Resolution left the Solar System. Then he went to work on the wireless system, and after an hour of testing, locating replacement parts, and plugging them in was rewarded by a small crab-like maintenance robot showing up, ready to work.

"Soup's on," Helen's voice rang down the narrow corridor to the engineering section. Jacques left the clean-up to the robot and pulled himself up the passageway.

By twenty-third century starship standards, the shuttle's berths, tiny mess and compact flight deck were cramped and utilitarian. But compared to how Jacques and company had been living for the last six months, they were the height of luxury.

Everyone but him had cycled through the tiny shower and gotten fresh shipsuits. Even Helen was wearing hers—she hadn't left all the cooking to the robotics.

"Go have your shower. It'll wait ten minutes," she said, and he complied. The head was a oval-cross-section marvel of spatial efficiency, with an improbably tiny combination commode and wash basin in one end and the shower in the other. He removed his clothes, stood on the grate, and let the doors close around him. Almost immediately, a warm hurricane descended on him, followed by a short needle spray that emerged from every direction, reached every crevice of his body, and was quickly sucked away. The cycle repeated twice automatically, and he had it repeat again. He emerged clean, dry, and somehow feeling both stimulated and exhausted.

When they all got together, before they dug in to a meal of real replicated Earth food, Helen said, "We've been really lucky. I'd like to do something to commemorate this. Maybe sing?"

Soob quickly scratched something on his slate and handed it to Helen.

"Amazing Grace," she read. "Very appropriate, I think. Do we all know it?"

Everyone nodded, and they began, led by Doc's deep baritone. Somehow, while he still couldn't talk, Soob was able to sing along, surprising himself as much as everyone else. Afterward, however, he still couldn't talk. They held off business until after their meal of gyros; everything replicated of course, but it tasted wonderful. Finally they sat and stared at each other.

"We still have a lot of work to do," Helen started. "We need a base of operations. We need to decide what to do about Gabe's group."

"We have a huge crime to deal with," Collette said, "dozens of dead or deprived..." She had difficulty finishing the sentence. "...of the lives they knew."

"Whoever the conspirators are, there are innocent people with them," Jacques said.

Helen looked as hard as he had ever seen her. "Just how innocent are the ones that chose to stay with Suretta and Eddie? Misogynist power-hungry charlatans. Anyone should see that. And how do you have a trial in a community this small, especially when you're a minority? They made their choice. Leave them to live, or die, with it."

"We haven't determined who was controlling the shuttle," Collette said, "nor if he, or she, or they were the saboteurs, nor if a saboteur was who murdered Ascendant Chryse. We probably need to do that, if we can, before contacting the rest of the survivors. And we need to keep up the shuttle deliveries of critical nutrients to avoid suspicion."

Doc chuckled. "Perhaps we simply see who's been meeting the shuttle."

Soob wrote, "Secure base first, take risks second."

Helen nodded. "It will be risky to make any deliveries at all; whoever did this may have a contingency plan."

Collette shook her head. "There is some risk, but to effectively execute all of them? That's more than I want on my conscience. Besides, I want to know what happened."

"How much time do we have?" Jacques asked. "When is the next resupply flight?"

"Resupply flights have been at random intervals, generally from six to ten days," the shuttle AI responded.

"Who orders them?" Collette asked.

"The identifier is: A5428C42."

"We need to see one of those meetings," Collette said. "I wonder if the security means they are guarding against us, or each other."

Helen laughed. "Somehow, I don't see Gabe anticipating that we'd tunnel through to where he's been hiding the shuttle."

"It might not be Gabe. Leo's more the type. Or maybe even one of the women, staying in the background. What are you thinking, Jacques?" Doc asked.

He was thinking they needed more time and less risk. "We could set up a minimum stand-alone facility at Eagles Nest—we can get there if things go sour with the shuttle. Then let things proceed until we have more information. When we know what we're dealing with and have a good fallback, we can decide the next step."

"To Eagles Nest!" Doc said.

"Not so fast," Jacques said. "If I was able to track the shuttle's position, whoever's been using it will as well. We shouldn't use if for transportation until we're ready."

∞◇∞

It was a good concept, Jacques thought, but it gave them only about five days to replicate the replicator. They stayed at "Tunnel's End" for the time being while the shuttle essentially "printed" three dimensional objects on a five by five centimeter stage. The device itself, with its power supply, input matter processor, cooling connections, and so on was almost half a cubic meter. That had to be "broken down" into five-centimeter cubed sections, and it wasn't designed that way. The AI helped, but it was well into the third day before the parts started coming out.

When the call came on the afternoon of the fourth day, it caught them unprepared.

"A5428C42 has directed a flight," *Fortitude* announced on Jacques' wrist comp; only he and Soob were in the vicinity. They quickly helped the robots get their things off.

The *Fortitude* came back, a day later to everyone's relief, especially Helen's.

"I got my necklace back!" she beamed.

But when they played back the recording of who was meeting the shuttle, they got a surprise. It was a tiny kangasaur that came aboard and picked up the bottle of nutrient powder from the replicator stage, then hopped away.

"Trained?" Doc speculated.

"Cute, anyway," Collette said. "I think it's a robot. Nobody would notice it, and our perp wouldn't need excuses for occasional long absences. But, a robot is unlikely to command the shuttle to do anything different, nor notice that the "Trojan" memory chip is no longer in charge."

"We need to proceed quickly; they're bound to be suspicious, eventually."

After two weeks working with the new replicator, they had a ten kilowatt boron-proton power plant, and a collapsible electric cart to make the trip back to Eagles Nest in a couple of days. Knowing what to look for, they found a vertical maintenance access to the Eagles Nest lava tube.

Another week gave them a second working replicator with a larger assembly platform at Eagles Nest. Tools, sanitary facilities, beds and small robots soon followed.

On the fourth return of the shuttle, they felt ready to visit the New Landing community. Soob got a dinosaur-capable tranquilizer dart gun. Collette got herself a complete police officer's kit. Everyone else got tranquilizer flechette pistols.

The call for the next shipment of nutrient powder came, and they all got aboard.

The view of Cube World from space was spectacular and bizarre. At the high point of their trajectory, they could see three faces, each with green, blue, and green concentric circles at its center.

"You're not wearing your necklace," Collette said to Helen as deceleration began. "Edith would love to see it!"

Helen beamed. "I'll get it right now so I don't forget it."

At a quarter gee, the deceleration provided no real hindrance to moving around the shuttle. They were almost down when she reemerged on the control deck.

"I couldn't find it," she said, deliberately. "Must have left it at Camp Fortitude."

Camp Fortitude? Jacques was suddenly alert—they'd never named any place "Camp Fortitude."

He turned and looked at her. Her eyes were wide and her face was grim. She raised a finger to her lips. Helen hadn't left her necklace anywhere but on the shuttle. On the shuttle Fortitude.

Which wasn't this; there were three shuttles to start with—identical, of course.

He looked at the others to see if they'd gotten the clue, and was answered by grim faces and grave nods. They had. They would have only seconds before this shuttle's hobbled brain realized they knew and disabled them. Soob took his slate and scratched on it: "gas hoods."

The shipsuits had hoods with clear visors packed in their collars. They would provide protection against a knockout gas, if that was what was intended for them. A quick look at the environmental systems display panel showed fan level at max—something was being blown into the command deck as fast as the shuttle's systems could send it. Without delay, Jacques released his hood, pulled it over his head, and sealed it at the neck. Soob had his on, too, as did Collette.

Doc and Helen weren't quite in time, and slumped, unconscious, in their seats as the spacecraft settled to the ground.

Collette was at the command deck hatch in a flash, and cranked it shut manually, while Jacques and Soob finished getting the hoods over Helen and Doc.

"This is *Resolution* Shuttle *Intrepid*. You are under arrest by order of the President of Providence. It is a crime to resist this order. It is also impossible as you will eventually run out of air. You must submit to the authority of Captain Suretta who will bring you into Providence."

# CHAPTER 18
# ON BEING BORN AGAIN

"**N**ot in your cybernetic life," Jacques said, and jumped over to the primary memory panel. It was locked, but he now had a laser tool, and quickly cut through its thin composite material. The sound of a torch working on the much more solid material of the command deck hatch reached him. He only had a few seconds.

He fumbled with the panel.

"I think we have about twenty seconds," Collette said, as she motioned the others into defensive positions. They would block the door as long as they could. Helen had found a roll of space tape, and taped over the cut as the robot cut it. It would take the torch only seconds to cut through that "repair," but those would be precious seconds.

Jacques turned back to his work and focused. Like the *Fortitude*, the *Intrepid* had been hacked with a single ersatz memory module. His fingers were like thumbs; the damn thing was stuck in, not budging. His fingers slipped off it, time and time again.

Screwdriver! He fumbled to find it in his tool kit. The torch stopped followed by loud bangs.

"Jacques," Collette yelled.

He had the screwdriver and pried at the module, ignoring thumps and curses behind him.

Then it broke free, and Jacques yanked it out.

Silence fell on the command deck. He turned to find his comrades covered with three or four maintenance robots each, stuck to them like crabs, covering their faces and hands. He felt something on his own back; he hadn't noticed it before. It had been that close.

"*Intrepid, this is Jacques Song...*" he said, beginning the same routine he'd used on the *Fortitude*. When he finished, the maintenance robots meekly abandoned their positions and skittered back to their stations. He found the backup modules, rebooted the AI, and summoned up a view of the shuttle's exterior.

Leo was standing near the entrance hatch. He obviously knew something was amiss; he had a gun out and was looking at his wrist comp and talking.

Collette stared at him. "Three shuttles. Of course. We knew that. We should have been asking ourselves where the others were."

"Just blast off right now, and we solve a whole bunch of problems," Helen said.

"Uh-uh," Collette said. "Bring him in. I've got a lot of questions."

"I think what Helen means," Doc said, "is that the whole question of governance, and thus the authority of anyone to imprison or try anyone else is very murky in these circumstances. The legal tradition is for settlements to elect their leadership. We, in essence, lost that election."

"This is not a colony, or an intentional settlement." Collette responded. "However removed, we are still part of a Solar System expedition, under the authority of the government that sent it."

Jacques watched Leo outside, pacing with increasing restiveness. Might he try to shoot his way in? "People, the alternative to us taking charge appears to be to allow mass murderers to run things. For now, Mr. Suretta waits outside with a gun. As Helen points out, to simply blast off with him in his present position would solve a lot of things. I'm not sure the shuttle AI will do that, however. Does anyone have any ideas about how to disable Mr. Suretta without doing him great bodily harm?"

"Do we still control *Fortitude*?" Helen asked. "Could its robots do something?"

"In an hour or so," Doc said. "It's on one of the other Cube World faces now."

Soob wrote furiously.

"We have 1 robot outside now," Helen read, with a puzzled look. Doc laughed. "Of course!"

∞◇∞

Half an hour later, they watched Leo Suretta collapse from a dart fired by a trank gun held by the miniature kangasaur that had been unloading the nutrient shipments.

Leo couldn't see both sides of the shuttle at once, and they'd gotten the trank gun out a maintenance door just big enough for Helen's arm, after they'd removed the intervening equipment.

With Lt. Collette's prisoner secured in one of the *Intrepid's* berths, they lifted off for New Landing, or "Providence" as Gabe had apparently renamed it. For good measure they contacted the *Fortitude*, and had it join them. The *Resolution's* shuttles set down on the beach on the north side of New Landing.

The place had grown, with several huts on stilts near the cave mouth, fish and laundry drying, on lines and a faint whiff of untreated sewage.

One would expect that two spaceships landing at this settlement of some stranded astronauts would have attracted some attention, Jacques thought. And it did. Everyone was open-mouthed except for Gabe. He sat down and cradled his head in his hands. Then he focused on Jacques.

"Where's Leo?" he asked, simply.

"In custody," Collette answered. "What was your role in all this?" she asked with a wave toward the shuttles.

"Leo woke me up before we hit this planet's atmosphere. He told me to be on the *Fortitude*," Gabe said, "and said the ship would notify the others. Look, this was a chance to go back to Eden. To get everything right. To live the way..."

"What others?" Collette demanded.

"I'm sorry about not telling you about the shuttles, but if y'all knew, you wouldn't have formed the community. You all would just try and build a starship to go back to something that was over and done with thousands of years ago. There's a way people were meant to be, and that's not part of it any more than what those New Reformationists were doing."

"What others?" Collette repeated.

"Leo, Evgenie and I were on one. There's a group over on the face east of here from the *Intrepid*. They're the control group; they know about the shuttles. The third shuttle crashed."

"Control group? You were running an experiment?" Doc sounded incredulous.

"I had some ideas about how to ease the New Reformationists back into the fold. I sort of adapted them to the situation."

"Which you helped engineer," Collette stated.

Gabe shook his head. "No, no. We were already here when Leo woke me up. We discussed how to handle things. He'd just found out and had some good ideas about how to handle this." He looked around at a sea of stony faces. "At least I thought so."

"Then it was Leo who disabled the homing lasers," Collette said, looking at her copcom.

She could probably tell if he believed what he was saying, Jacques thought.

Gabe looked absolutely miserable. "I don't know that for a fact."

"Let's say I believe you. The circumstantial evidence is overwhelming."

"Leo sabotaged the deceleration mechanism at 36 Ophiuchi?" Maria Lopes questioned. "He wouldn't do that! He's a good man! Where is he?"

No one said anything for several minutes. This was going to be very difficult, Jacques knew.

"He's in custody," Collette said. Slowly and carefully, she took Maria through everything Leo had done, from the initial sabotage and his efforts to see that only a select group of reliable people were on the shuttles to keeping their existence from the rest of the survivors at the price of letting Jacques' group go off to what they thought would be certain death.

"How are you going to have a trial?" Gabe asked. "What are you going to do, hang him?"

"Maybe we'll think of something," Doc offered. "What about Ascendant's murder?"

Gabe wasn't looking at him. He was looking up at the path down from the Rim, and pointing with a shaking finger at the end of a shaking arm. A lone woman in what looked to be a shipsuit was walking down the path from the rim.

"Do you believe in ghosts?" Gabe asked, pointing to a woman walking down the path. Then he laughed hysterically. "'Cause if you do you all can ask *her*."

The woman descending the path looked exactly like Ascendant Chryse.

# CHAPTER 19
# BEYOND CRIME AND
# JUSTICE

"There's nothing to fear," she said as she reached the group and touched a shuddering Gabe. "I'm flesh and blood, nothing supernatural."

"Whoever built this world... rebuilt you?" Doc asked.

"I'm not a robot, Doc. The caretaker's nanites recorded my brain and my DNA. Its replicators are somewhat more advanced than ours." She grinned. "I'm missing some memories, some scars, and I'll need to work on a tan."

"But you are a mind reader, now, it seems," he said, smiling slightly.

"I made a good guess," she answered. "Though the latter is possible, if we want to do it."

We. Jacques shuddered. Whatever ran this place apparently could replicate whatever it chose, which did not surprise him too greatly, and had the willingness to use it in this fashion, which did.

"Are you really Ascendant Chryse?" he asked.

"I certainly feel like me, but thanks for saving the diary, Jacques. I went to sleep in my CSU and woke up at Rim Camp. But, and this will be difficult to explain; I'm much more than me."

"More? Who, or what, are you... now?" Doc asked.

"On a time scale of milliseconds, my awareness extends to this entire world; on a time scale of hours, this entire planetary system; on a time scale of decades, all the stars human beings have settled; on a time scale of millennia, a part of an arm of the Milky Way and the wisdom of ten thousand races; and on a time scale of hundreds of millennia, the collective culture of our galaxy. But there's more. I compass a heritage of races including some now beyond the horizon of space and time–though, and I can only explain this in metaphor, the far horizon is quite misty."

"Intelligent life may be the universe's way of becoming conscious," Collette said in hushed tones. "Or something like that. I can't remember who said that–hundreds of years ago."

"Carl Sagan, on Earth. Also by millions of other beings on millions of other planets," Ascendant said.

Soob pulled his slate out of his bag, scratched on it, and showed the others what he wrote: *Did you meet God?* He handed it to Ascendant.

Ascendant smiled and kissed Soob on the forehead. "Feel better?"

"Very much," Soob said. "Oh, my..."

"God," she said. "The word 'meet' doesn't quite do justice to my present circumstance. Tell me, does it make a great difference to you that I did this with nanocells rather than some supernatural force?"

Soob took a long time to respond. "In a philosophical sense, a very profound difference, in a practical sense... perhaps none at all."

Gabriel Eddie sat on a rock and covered his face with his hands. Evgenie, Arroya, Maria and Dominic gathered around him. Edith stood, staring at Ascendant.

"There's a net here?" Doc asked. "I don't sense anything."

"Different frequencies and protocols," Ascendant said. "We'll fix that later."

"Are you an individual or part of a collective mind?" Helen asked.

"The question itself assumes categories which don't really apply," Ascendant answered. "Our language requires me to use singular or plural pronouns, thus misleading you greatly. The sort of isolation which you experience, and I did, before my... change... is a very primitive characteristic by galactic standards, a stage that many races went through and most passed beyond."

"When we left the Solar System," Collette said, "most philosophers ascribed the lack of contact with other civilizations to a very strong quarantine, an ethic much like that of our own environmentalists that forbids interference with nature."

Ascendant smiled. "But that can't go on forever, can it?"

Jacques nodded. "Eventually, we would start impacting other civilizations. We've probably screwed things up here, ecologically, haven't we? As I'm sure you know, that was not the choice of any of the individuals here."

"You have killed sentient beings to keep your individual selves alive. In most of the galaxy, that would be regarded as a very primitive characteristic in a spacefaring race. As people, we are still driven by emotions, needs to dominate, reproduce, preserve ourselves. Most of the universe has moved beyond that."

"So, the caretaker of this world does nothing? Just watches us suffer."

"Think of all the life forms that feel, hurt, need, and suffer and all the gradations of awareness. Suffering can't all be banished, but it can have meaning from what comes later. We were left–allowed–to solve our problems by ourselves."

"What changed? Why were you resurrected? Why contact us now?"

Ascendant giggled. "I'm still human enough to enjoy this. Dear, dear, Jacques. We, the human race, solved our problems. We're out of the cradle and off the rug, so to speak. Just taking baby steps, mind you, but it's time for humanity to learn the rules."

"Humanity?" Doc asked. "Does your, uh, expanded awareness have some news from the solar system?"

She nodded. "There's a lot to talk about. Have you seen the new star in the sky?"

"Near Antares," Jacques said. "We have to catch it just before Antares rise, or the glare hides it."

"It's a starship decelerating. The solar system has found you. They'll be here in a few months."

∞◇∞

It was a clear, still, dry evening and exceptionally cool for their altitude. The women of Providence, perhaps sensing that their way of life was to change unalterably again, made the best of things by putting on a feast around the campfire. The shuttles replicated some wine and beer–the first spirits any of them had tasted for six subjective months, or a thousand years of real time.

So fortified, with Ascendant's help, they caught up, at least to circa 2800 CE. Earth still maintained a stable constitutional monarchy, but that was for tradition and show; AI's did everything and the only person with a real job was the Empress. The ancient effort to rescue the 36 Ophiuchi colony had been successful, if one could call the thousands of deaths that involved a success. It was the last such effort ever attempted.

Human-derived colonies still, occasionally, did some horrendous things, but the Universe had better ways of dealing with that. Nanites invaded bodies and changed minds.

Humans had made a black hole, and now had hundreds of them powering space colonies, performing physics experiments, and generally being useful. The initial effort had drawn the attention of passing spacefarers of an ancient, but conservative-by-choice branch of a civilization of flying aliens. Not long after that, a galactic library node had been discovered in Neptune's moon, Proteus. So, well before the *Resolution* hit Cube World, humanity had found its way into the galactic community.

Ascendant concluded by saying that she might very well be a common example of the human-descended beings they would encounter in the Galaxy today, but the variety was wide.

Gabe said, "I knew we'd be a group of Rip van Winkles, but *this*... this will take a whole lot of digesting."

Ascendant laughed, as did a number of others, at first timidly, then heartily. What Ascendant was telling them was hard to grasp, but Gabe was clearly finding it harder than most.

Jacques added, "And we are still six hundred years behind the times."

"Or ahead of them, depending on which way the information is flowing," Helen noted. "I imagine this story will still make a splash on Earth!"

"Are we welcome here?" Arroya Montez asked. "Do we have to go back? I have a very simple, stable life here, with Evgenie. My knowledge is all out of date, and I would have no place on Earth, now."

Ascendant smiled at her. Jacques thought there might have been something like recognition in her expression. But she gave no hint of it as she answered Montez' question.

"This world is an experiment in evolution. Six identical environments and with identical seed stock, constructed by beings not too unlike your 'kangasaur' about half a billion years ago, a race not entirely given to theory and abstractions.

"What, they wondered, if one reran evolution for real; would the Universe produce anything like them again? So they put it to the real test. It's been running about two hundred fifty million years. The cube shape is a bit of whimsy, or art. But it's also functional; the biospheres remain isolated and the long slide of basalt down the cube edges face drives the tectonics that recycle this world's carbon."

"Our landing must have upset things," Doc said.

"Like the KT impact on Earth?" Soob remarked. "Contingencies, like us, are what drives evolutionary change."

Ascendant laughed. "Yes, all grist for the mill. The caretaker takes it in stride."

"We aren't going to get kicked off?" Dominic asked. "We can stay here?"

"It is a bit unusual. In the quarter billion years Cube World has existed, only 1,728 other intelligent races have stumbled upon it before their incorporation into galactic society. Twenty-three hundred years is the longest any of them have stayed. The resurfacing time is about fifty-seven thousand years. Now, the beings Jacques calls "dinotowers" have long memories, but there is no other trace of these visitations in any of the biospheres. You're welcome to stay a while as long as you control your numbers."

Gabe shook his head. "Do we want to? My God says I shall have no other gods before 'im. I'm not sure where alien planet-ruling machines fits into that."

"You'd probably find Earthmind quite a shock, then," Ascendant said. "It's a virtual universe for people who tire of biology."

"Oh, Lord," Gabe sighed. "Were we wrong? Or... were we right?"

Ascendant smiled. "Here, you'll be left alone as much as you wish, while you figure that out."

"Maybe that's good for now, Gabe," Maria said.

"We still have some formalities of justice to consider," Collette declared.

"Judge not," Gabe said softly, "lest ye be judged."

Everyone was silent.

"What does justice mean now?" Soob finally asked. "What purpose is there in punishment? I suppose one wants to do something to ensure that a perpetrator doesn't act obnoxiously in the future. Even if murder, or should I say attempted murder, is futile here, I would think it would still be quite an inconvenience. The whole point of this galactic ethical structure seems to be that beings, as collective races, I suppose, have a right to seek their own destiny."

Ascendant laughed. "Not badly put. While I am very comfortable with who I am now, it is true that I would not have chosen this experience for myself. But as for what you do about Leo, we human beings can be human beings as long as we don't... greatly inconvenience... others."

"Or until we decide to be something else?" Helen asked.

Ascendant nodded. "It seems fairly certain that you will, eventually. But there's no hurry and will certainly be no coercion."

"I'd always feel someone is watching over my shoulder," Helen said.

"A new feeling for an atheist, I'd guess," Gabe said, reviving a bit.

"Did Leo kill you, Ascendant?" Doc asked.

She smiled with a shake of her head. "Not for lack of trying. Leo Suretta, or Leo Syrtis, as he was named at birth on Mars, was the New Reformation's agent on the *Resolution*. It was supposed to be a martyrdom mission, for him, murder for the rest of us–or perhaps an act of war. But I was up, and managed to restore the AI and wake the command team in time to devise and implement the contingency plan. We found this place, so Leo saw an opportunity to create another authoritarian culture." Ascendant sighed. "He arranged for people he thought would make the kind of society he wanted to be on the shuttles."

"The CSUs were safer," she concluded. "There was no guarantee the shuttles would survive the hundred-kilometer-per-second crash into Cube World's atmosphere. One of them, the *Purpose*, did not. Leo thought the gamble was worth it. A megalomaniac's collateral damage."

Maria sobbed.

"But," Collette said, diverting attention from her, "Leo's sabotage didn't kill Ascendant, and neither did Gabe–they hadn't arrived on our island when that happened. Her CSU log wasn't wiped until later, right Gabe?"

Gabe nodded. "Leo didn't want problems about how we got here confusin' people about what to do now that we were here."

"Ascendant, do you know who turned off your CSU power, while you slept?"

"Actually, I don't. We are all scanned, but only every few nights. The caretaker didn't happen to be watching."

"No matter. I think I know. There were two shuttles," Collette said. "Leo and Gabe were on one, and on the other…"

Arroya Montez quietly tried to slip away from the fire, thus assuring that all eyes fell on her. Evgenie got up to go after her.

"Arroya," Ascendant called after her "I'm not dead, so there is no murder and I assure you I am no danger to your happiness with Evgenie. Be at peace. I forgive you."

Gabe groaned, "Now, come on, you're tryin' to sound like…"

Their eyes locked and Gabe's face lost its color. Very slowly, he asked, "That whatchyoucallit, library node, they found in the solar system. It hasn't been there three thousand years or so, has it?"

"More like three million, Gabe." Ascendant wasn't smiling.

Gabe fell silent. Jacques imagined an orchestra playing *Also Sprach Zarathustra*.

"How far back does the oldest part of you go?" Doc asked. "When did the universe become conscious?"

"The eldest we know of came from a planet about a star much like this one in a dwarf galaxy now beyond the universal expansion event horizon. They were much closer nine billion years ago, and spread their–I think "culture" would be the best word–far and wide. Their ethics became the model for everyone since; though great minds have thought alike in this area.

"Speaking of ethics, Jacques, Leo should be here."

Jacques nodded, contacted the *Intrepid* and directed that its robots bring Leo to the gathering, unrestrained. No one had anything to fear from him, not ever again.

When he arrived, he looked at Gabe, Jacques, and then, tight-lipped, at Ascendant.

"I'm Ascendant Chryse," she said.

"The shuttle told me." Leo's voice was tense, his tone, defiant.

"We know everything," Collette said.

"You may forgive yourself, in time," Doc said.

Leo snorted. "Forgive myself? I'm proud of what I tried, damn it. I tried to save mankind from this damned, banal, inhuman fate. I tried at 36 Ophiuchi and I tried here. You aren't human, Chryse. You're not more than human, you're less. You're an abomination, an alien puppet."

Leo pulled out a gun; he apparently had a stash of them somewhere, Jacques realized.

Doc laughed. As the others realized the futility of Leo's weapon they began to laugh as well. Except Ascendant, who looked very sad.

"Yeah, real funny," Leo said. "Well, I'm betting you aliens are just too damned civilized for eternal torture. I quit."

He turned the gun on himself. Nobody made a move or said a thing to stop him. He managed to fire five times before collapsing.

Everyone looked at Ascendant. She had a tear in her eye. "I could have done something, but I am informed that wisdom lies in respecting his wishes. He won't be revived; that *would* be torture."

# CHAPTER 20
## AS IN THE BEGINNING

**B**efore they left for the Solar System, Jacques and Collette visited Face One a last time. With power-assisted wings, they covered the distance in three days, reliving adventures and overnighting at Rim Camp and River Camp, before ending up at Ascendant Chryse's lodge near Eagles Nest. Soob, Helen, Doc and their children were there. The oldest, Athena, was now approaching puberty, and as clever as her mother.

"Are you sure?" Jacques asked Ascendant.

Ascendant put her arms around him, acknowledging that in some alternative existence, and perhaps some future one, they were soulmates.

"This is where I belong now," she said. "We need to develop a different view perspective of time; by Galactic standards, I am really not so far away. Besides, I'm pregnant!"

Soob was grinning ear from ear. "I'm going to enjoy exploring the other cube faces and renewing acquaintances with other ressurectees."

"And someone needs to keep the fear of God in Gabe," Helen added.

Doc chuckled. "Gabe enjoys leading, and the people with him enjoy being led. Their first generation is just coming of age. I'll enjoy watching them rebel."

"The galactic data base here is larger than the library node in the solar system," Helen said, "and with my family, I'm really happy. So come back in a couple of millennia!"

Then they said their farewells, Collette took his hand, perhaps a bit firmly, and led him back to the Fortitude. Hours later, with them aboard, *Resolution II* picked up the beam to Earth.

Within a day, Cube World's star shrank noticeably. When it dimmed to about the same apparent luminosity as Antares, they made love once more, then entered their CSUs. Years later, they revived briefly to gape at the glowing red mist of the supergiant star as its gravity bent them toward Earth. But it too dwindled, and Jacques made one last check of his enhanced emergency kit and permitted the CSU's transparent lid to settle down over him for the six-hundred-year journey. For him, the thirty-third century had ended, and the thirty-ninth would soon begin.


The End... of a Beginning.

Visit
briefcandlepress.com
to read about the author,
the science behind some of his stories,
and upcoming publications

www.ingramcontent.com/pod-product-compliance
Lightning Source LLC
Chambersburg PA
CBHW030230180626
46810CB00008B/3059